Praise for

Winner of the Costa Children's Book Award 2019
Winner of the Times Children's Fiction Competition 2017
Chosen as one of the Guardian's best children's books of 2019
Shortlisted for the Waterstones Children's Book Prize 2020

'This book is such a light-filled, huge-hearted delight of an adventure.'
KATHERINE RUNDELL

'A beautifully evocative adventure, complete with prowling tigers
and mystical vultures, that follows a young girl's journey
through the Himalayas to find her father.'
ABI ELPHINSTONE

'This jewel of a book, suffused with colour, warmth, hope and, of course,
edge-of-your-seat adventure, is the perfect holiday read.
Every school should have a copy.'
LAUREN ST JOHN

'High stakes set against a vividly evoked setting, steeped in wild mysticism.
I was swept along by Asha's story from the first page.'
SARAH DRIVER

'An evocative debut novel . . . satisfyingly classic in feel.'
THE GUARDIAN

'. . . a heartfelt and mystical children's adventure story.'
THE TELEGRAPH

'. . . weaves themes of faith, friendship and greed into a vibrant
adventure with a rich seam of magic realism.'
THE BOOKSELLER

'[A] warm, comforting story . . . the final ending
is as perfect as any fairy tale.'

A MESSAGE FROM CHICKEN HOUSE

Tamarind never knew her Indian mum. Now, she's visiting her ancient ancestral home for the first time, uncovering a family feud, and a long-buried secret tangled up in the huge, overgrown gardens. Here she finds friendship, jealousy and a mystical guiding hand leading her to the truth about what happened in the past . . . and how the future can be healed. Jasbinder Bilan is a brilliant new talent who mingles a mystical magical realism with all the warmth and compassion of real life. She wanted me not to forget to mention the monkey – a helper in more ways than one. There, I did!

BARRY CUNNINGHAM
Publisher
Chicken House

JASBINDER BILAN

TAMARIND & THE STAR OF ISHTA

Chicken House

2 Palmer Street, Frome, Somerset BA11 1DS
www.chickenhousebooks.com

Text © Jasbinder Bilan 2020
Cover illustration © Aitch 2020

First published in Great Britain in 2020
Chicken House
2 Palmer Street
Frome, Somerset BA11 1DS
United Kingdom
www.chickenhousebooks.com

Cover and interior design by Helen Crawford-White
Cover illustration by Aitch
Map illustration © Alexis Snell 2020
Typeset by Dorchester Typesetting Group Ltd
Printed and bound in Great Britain by CPI Group (UK) Ltd, Croydon CR0 4YY

The paper used in this Chicken House book is made
from wood grown in sustainable forests.

3 5 7 9 10 8 6 4

British Library Cataloguing in Publication data available.

PB ISBN 978-1-913322-17-5
eISBN 978-1-913322-48-9

This book is dedicated to my dearest mum, Gurjinder, who knows what it means to grow up without a mother and has opened her beautiful heart to everyone.

TAMARIND'S MATERNAL FAMILY TREE

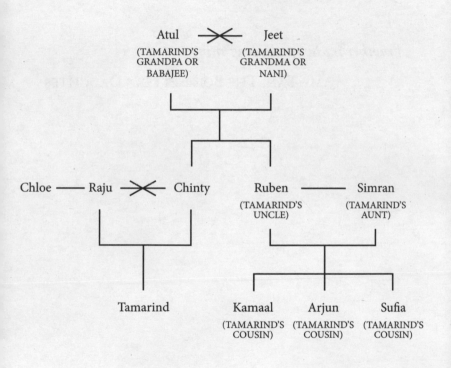

Atul ✕ Jeet
(TAMARIND'S GRANDPA OR BABAJEE) (TAMARIND'S GRANDMA OR NANI)

Chloe — Raju ✕ Chinty   Ruben — Simran
(TAMARIND'S UNCLE) (TAMARIND'S AUNT)

Tamarind

Kamaal   Arjun   Sufia
(TAMARIND'S COUSIN) (TAMARIND'S COUSIN) (TAMARIND'S COUSIN)

A mother is always the beginning.

AMY TAN, THE BONESETTER'S DAUGHTER

1

There's a small photo I keep on my bedside table; it's old and crinkly with a neat fold along the left-hand corner. In the photo Mum's about my age, but I can't really tell if I look like her because the photograph's taken from a long way off. She's on a home-made swing and it's fixed to a huge tree in full blossom. Her legs are waving in the air, and behind her I can just make out a house with a verandah all around it. I love this photo because Mum's full of life, but it makes me cry that I never got to know her or hold her hand or snuggle into her shoulder.

It's the only thing of Mum's that Dad would let me have, the last gift she ever gave him, and I'm keeping it safe for both of us.

I don't know what happened to Mum, Dad won't tell me much – all he'll say is she was poorly, and died when I was a baby. But now, for the first time, I'm going to find out. The thing is, I'm not sure I want to. I slip Mum's photo from the back of my passport and hold it in my palm, shuffle away from Chloe and turn to face the aeroplane window. I don't want her quizzing me again, asking me more questions about how I'm feeling. Being all motherly.

I flick her a quick look but she doesn't see; she carries on reading, absorbed in the book, long blond hair hiding her freckled face. Do we look like a family when we're out together? Me and Dad with our golden skin; Chloe, who goes raspberry red at the sight of the sun?

Dad leans across, taps me on the shoulder. 'Mint?' he asks, shoving a bag of sweets under my nose. 'We'll be landing in Rinigaar soon, and remember about ears popping?'

My stomach turns a double somersault when I think about staying with Mum's family all by myself. I hold Dad's gaze, plead with his warm brown eyes that everyone tells me are just like mine, and hope he's going to change his mind about leaving me there alone. He pulls a funny face and his dimples appear.

Chloe puts her book down and digs into the mints. 'Mmmm . . . these are yum. Have one, Tam, they haven't got any gelatine in. I double-checked.' She smiles at Dad and glances down at the photo.

I move further towards the window and slide the photo away, putting everything back in my green Scandi rucksack.

'Dad always gets the ones without gelatine.' I take a mint and put it in my mouth.

Chloe ties back her hair and fiddles with her wedding ring. 'I've been learning a few new veggie recipes too. I think it's great to eat less meat.'

I keep looking out of the window. When she was just Dad's girlfriend, we were OK, but ever since they married and she moved in, it's been so different. I know she's my new mum now, but what does that even mean? And lately I just can't seem to be nice to her.

Dad's voice jolts me from my worries. 'Tamarind. Chloe's talking to you.'

I try to swallow the lump that's been burning my throat since we set off on this journey. If I was still five, I'd jump up and down and throw my things around, maybe even scream until Dad calmed me down, but instead I curl even further towards the window, stare at the clouds that stretch on and on and the blue sky above them. 'Thank you,' I croak.

Would Mum have checked my food for gelatine? Would she have loved me even through my tantrums?

I've thought about Mum my whole life, even though she hasn't been there: I've never given her daffodils on Mother's Day or made her a special card. There's a painful space inside me, and the closer we get to India and the family she left behind, the more tangled it's feeling.

Dad gives me his stern face. 'Let's go for a little walk.' He nods at Chloe. 'We won't be long.'

My stomach churns. I scoot past Chloe and follow Dad towards the loos at the back of the plane.

He holds my shoulders gently and stoops so our faces are close. 'I know this is hard, Tam.'

I feel my face flush, take a long breath and chew the edge of my thumb.

'I know you're scared, but everything will be OK. Chloe just wants to be the best mum to you . . . give her a chance.'

I kick at the carpet with the toe of my trainer, close my eyes and blink away the tears that have been waiting to fall. 'What happened to my real mum? I need to know.' I brush my cheeks roughly with the back of my hand. 'I'll be meeting the family any minute and I still don't know a thing. What did she die of?'

Dad's face softens but he doesn't answer my question. 'Take a deep breath.' He pulls me towards him

8

and gives me a big hug. He smells of mints and after-shave, washing powder and home.

It's like he wants me to forget my question – but I don't give up. 'I need to know a bit more than *I met Mum while I was backpacking in the Himalaya*,' I mumble into his shirt. I push him away. 'I want to know what she was *like*. Please. It's your job to tell me!'

'Look. Your mum loved you to bits, and one day when you're a bit older I'll tell you everything, but for the moment . . .' He pushes his fingers through his hair. 'I don't want to upset you.'

But it seems to me like he's the one who's getting upset.

2

Once the plane has landed I try to get my jittery insides in order, but they keep knotting up. I feel I'm being thrown into a firepit of the unknown; meeting Mum's family for the first time, seeing India, the place where I was born. I don't know if I can do it all by myself.

We collect our cases and Dad leads us through into the main part of the airport. I wish he would slow down but he's striding ahead, looking for the family. I hurry along the slippery floor after Dad, my wheelie case swooshing behind me, trying to keep up. The air is so thick I can hardly breathe, and it's so noisy. I have to keep pulling at my clothes to stop the heat sticking them to my skin.

'There they are.' Dad heads off again, towards a woman dressed in a purple sari with gold embroidery along the edge. She's got a happy smile on her face and is looking right at me, waving both arms in the air to catch our attention. Beside her is a boy a bit younger than me. He's wearing long blue shorts with trainers and an orange T-shirt with a drawing of a skateboarder on it. He's staring at the ground but as we approach he holds up a huge handwritten sign:

Welcome to India, Tamarind

It brings me out in an instant embarrassed rash and I duck behind Dad.

'It'll be fine, Tamarind,' says Chloe, hooking her arm through mine. 'We'll be back before you know it.'

I wriggle free from her and accidentally kick my case. 'Ow . . .'

'Careful, Tam,' says Dad, shepherding me towards the sign.

How could they do this to me? How would *they* feel, being dumped off with strangers in a foreign country and left to it? This horrible mess is all Chloe's fault.

I mean, what am I going to say to people I've never met before? A whole week alone with them and I don't even speak Punjabi. The thought suddenly occurs to me with horror – maybe they don't speak any English!

Suddenly, I'm standing in front of them and

11

they're smiling at me, so even though I don't want to do what Dad taught me, I put my hands together, and find myself saying, '*Sat sri akaal,*' not sure if they understand my English Punjabi accent.

The boy puts his hand up to his mouth and giggles. 'Nice try! High five,' he says in perfect English, giving me a cheesy grin as he holds up his palm. My cheeks go hot – it wasn't *that* funny, was it? 'I'm Arjun, welcome to India,' he says, his hand dropping when I don't play along. He's only about nine and it doesn't look like we'll have anything in common.

Dad laughs at how embarrassed I am. I shoot him a glare and he wraps his arm around me. 'Sorry, Tam.' I pull away and his face falls, but I don't care. I'm hurting way more than he is.

'I'm your Aunt Simran,' the woman in purple interrupts. She turns her back to Dad and carries on speaking, but only to me, which I think is a bit rude. Doesn't she like Dad? 'You know, your mum's brother's wife. And this cheeky boy is my son – don't pay any attention to his teasing.' She holds out her arms but I don't step in for a hug. She drops her arms awkwardly. 'You've come such a long way . . . at last we get to see you. Let me look. Such beautiful long hair and this nice . . . football kit.' She gives Dad a

12

quick look, then turns her back to him again.

My fingers find Mum's photo in my pocket and feel for the comforting fold in the corner.

'You OK, Tam?' asks Chloe.

I just stare at the floor, willing myself not to lose it, wishing that Dad was coming with me. But I'm not sure he would be welcome – Aunt Simran is acting really weird towards him. Besides, I know he's waited so long for a honeymoon; it's been six months since he and Chloe got married. He deserves this break.

'Thank you, Simran, for coming all this way to collect Tamarind,' says Dad, clearing his throat. 'It will be good for her to meet you all at last, hey?'

'Don't worry, Raju.' Aunt Simran gives Dad a stiff little hug. 'We're family, no matter how long it's been.'

'We brought you some presents.' Chloe bounces up to Arjun and stuffs a bag bursting at the seams with British sweets into his arms. 'We'd better go – our train's leaving in an hour.'

Dad gives me one of his massive bear hugs and whispers, 'Only a week and I'll be back. They've been looking forward to seeing you for such a long time, try and enjoy it.'

'But, Dad . . .' I wipe my palms against my

Arsenal T-shirt. 'What am I going to eat? What if everything's too . . . too different?'

'I already told them in the letter. And I put a few things in your bag. In case of emergency.' He smiles.

I don't know if that makes me feel better or worse. I wipe my cheek against Dad's shirt.

'You'll be OK, Tam,' he says softly.

'I don't have much choice, do I?' I turn away from him to face the family.

'We'll be back before you know it,' says Chloe, stroking my cheek. 'We haven't forgotten it's your birthday on Sunday.'

I move away quickly, leaving Chloe's hand dangling in mid-air, and just catch her look at Dad.

'Bye then,' she says.

'Bye,' I mumble.

They trundle off into the distance, Dad shooting me a quick glance before they begin running to catch their train, and I think I might collapse right here, I feel so hot and strange.

'No worrying, OK?' Aunt Simran pulls me towards her. 'We'll look after you very well, promise.'

3

I try to stop my lip quivering as we bustle out of the airport and I'm smacked in the face by the most raucous place I've ever been. My head spins faster than a carousel and as I step backwards into the road, I narrowly miss being squashed by a meandering white cow.

Aunt Simran grabs me by the arm, pulling me back to the pavement. 'You'll get used to this,' says Arjun. 'It helps to have eyes in the back of your head, though.'

Cars, people, motorbikes and animals are sprawling everywhere. Starlings lined up along the telephone wires chatter mockingly. I feel for the phone in my pocket . . . is it too late to call Dad back?

A blue people carrier pulls up alongside us. The window winds down and blasts us with noisy drumbeats.

'Nice to meet you, Tamarind. I'm Kamaal,' says the young man in the driver's seat.

'That's my big brother. You won't see much of him,' says Arjun. 'He thinks he's a proper musician, hangs out with friends down here in the city mostly.' He leaps into the back seat of the car as my aunt climbs into the front.

I grab the hot metal door handle and slide into the car beside Arjun. It's so strange being here . . . I'm entering Mum's world all alone. I take a deep breath of cooled air.

'Are you from London then?' Arjun asks, nodding at my T-shirt.

'No,' I reply slowly. 'We live in Bristol, but my favourite football team is Arsenal. My all-time favourite player is Alex Scott.'

Arjun gives me a blank look.

'She used to play in the women's team – *and* for England – but now she's on telly, commentating on the World Cup and stuff. She's amazing. Dad took me to see her play once and I've been practising my dribbling ever since.' I'm speaking really fast, but Arjun doesn't seem to notice.

'Cool! I'm into skateboarding and origami but not at the same time,' he laughs, his eyes sparkling.

I'm warming to our conversation now. 'I was

16

meant to go to a summer camp . . . at Arsenal, I mean, with my best friend Rafi.' I swallow, my stomach suddenly plummeting. 'But I'm here instead.'

'Maybe you'll get to do it a different time,' he says, getting a small gamer out from the back of the seat in front. 'Want a go?'

I shake my head. 'Thanks, though.' I stare out of the window.

He fires it up and starts punching at the keys. 'I need to beat my record.'

A sad, empty feeling settles around me. All I can think of is Mum. It's as if she's flown from the photo and is everywhere I look, like she's right here beside me. I can't get her out of my mind and, although I never knew her, I miss her so much. I've never felt quite like this before.

Outside, the tall trees that line the road sway in the warm breeze. We drive alongside a wide river, cars and buses bumper to bumper, the air noisy with horns. In the far distance, snow-capped mountains rise into the turquoise-blue sky. The moon appears from behind one of the peaks and a bright star sits beside it, even though it's not dark yet. Further away the clouds begin to turn grey.

Arjun glances out of the window. 'Hope we don't get caught in a storm. It's monsoon season and that means rain.' He raps on the back of the driver's seat. 'Put your foot down, Kamaal.'

'Careful driving,' adds Aunt Simran. 'We have our lovely Tamarind with us.' She turns and smiles.

'Don't worry,' says Kamaal. 'I'll get everyone home safely.'

'Er . . . Aunt Simran,' I say, leaning forward. 'Will you tell me about Mum?'

She touches my hair. '*Beta*, not now, OK? It's a day for celebration, not sad things.'

I let the butterflies in my stomach fizzle to nothing, stare out of the window again.

Arjun shoots me a smile, angles his gamer towards me. 'Sure you don't want a go?'

I shake my head. The phone in my bag buzzes and I make a grab for it. A message from Rafi.

Hey Tam – When U back? Arsenal is sick but not same without U Call me!!!!!

I quickly tap my reply and send it off.

Message failed to send

Oh, what?! No mobile signal. I fling the phone into my bag, a lonely feeling creeping into my whole body.

We skirt around a vast green lake with houseboats

18

bobbing along its surface. A long-legged white bird swoops low across the water and dives in, reappearing a few moments later with a bright silver fish held tight in its beak.

We leave the busy streets and begin to climb away from the chaos of the city on hushed winding roads that wrap around the mountains, the car hugging close to the curves.

Small villages with houses perched at steep angles appear now and then, and bearded brown goats wander randomly along the road. It's getting cooler and quieter the further we drive, the sky turning the darkest pink I've ever seen.

We drive on and on until daylight begins to fade and each twist of the rough mountainous road takes us higher and higher towards the sharp snow-covered peaks. Eventually Arjun stops playing his game, his head sagging against the window as his eyes flutter shut.

A scattering of lone houses form a line along a dirt track, their silhouettes black against the last of the sun's rays. 'Final stretch,' says Kamaal, yawning.

We turn off the road and carry on driving along a stony track, climbing higher still, leaving the houses way behind. Owl calls screech through the open windows as we bump deeper into the darkness of the countryside.

'How much longer?' asks Arjun, waking up and rubbing his eyes.

'Nearly there,' replies Kamaal, finally slowing the people carrier down.

'You must be so tired, Tamarind,' says Aunt Simran. 'But you're here now, that's the important thing.'

Here. In the middle of the biggest nowhere I've ever seen, with a bunch of strangers. I grip the edge of my seat as a wave of panic surges through me. Where's Dad when I need him most?

We grind to a halt.

'*Alakapuri,*' I murmur, reading the carved wooden sign fixed to the old iron gates.

Kamaal leaps out of the car and creaks the gates open.

'Welcome,' says Aunt Simran, catching me staring at the sign. 'The house is named after the mythical Himalayan city of Alakapuri.'

'Oh.' What sort of house gets named after a mythical city?

We carry on in the car up a cobbled sweeping driveway, towards a large yellow moon hanging in the dark sky. We follow the tiny white lights lining the drive and finally come to a stop below a house . . .

it's *the* house, the one in the photo, although it's huge, much bigger than it seemed in the tiny picture. I can't stop staring at the impressive building perched high on a grassy mound.

The car doors whoosh open and a cold wind rushes in, blowing damp leaves into the car. Arjun sprints away, up the steps to the house, Kamaal following close behind.

But something makes me hesitate.

I hear music nearby, like a faint tune hummed on the wind, and I think I hear a word . . . *Tamarind*. I glance around into the shadowy garden, swallowing the cool night air. Who sang my name? Or was it just the wind? My heart begins to beat against my ribs.

Aunt Simran cradles my arm as she guides me down from the car. 'Big jump, Tamarind,' she says. 'You're shaking! Poor *beta*. It's been such a long journey, we need to get you inside. Come on.'

We walk slowly across crunching gravel, Aunt Simran still holding my arm. It's dark but the moon is bright and sheds its yellow light over the house. The domed turrets make it look almost like a palace. It sits high up on its mound, with the verandah running all around it and shutters pulled firmly across the windows.

'Can we stop a minute, please?' I ask.

'What is it?' Aunt Simran asks, pausing at my side.

I strain my eyes towards the gardens that drop away steeply and surround the house. The huge mountains loom in the distance, like a barrier against the world beyond and I can't shift that lonely feeling. The air is heavy with the strange smells of flowers and other plants I don't recognize, sharp, bitter and floral all at once.

I search the semi-darkness for the tree, the tree with the swing on it – Mum's tree.

But I can't see it anywhere.

A high-pitched scream rattles through the dark velvet night. 'W-what's that?'

'It's nothing,' says Aunt Simran. 'Let's get you inside.'

4

I stumble up the sweeping stone steps, Aunt Simran leading the way. At the top the front door is open and we step into a big hallway with a mosaicked floor. Large table lamps give off a cosy glow, lighting up paintings of tigers and deer on the walls.

I had no idea Mum lived in such a grand house and I feel even more out of place. It's a bit of a change from our little house back in Bristol. I close my eyes and conjure up its views over the park, the treehouse Dad made for me when I was six, where Rafi and I still have sleepovers in summer.

Arjun and Kamaal have already disappeared some-where – I can hear footsteps and low voices upstairs. Further along the corridor there's the echoing sound of pans clanking.

'I've put you in your mum's old room,' smiles Aunt Simran. 'I thought you'd like that.'

A shadow shoots across the floor, shapes flit in the corners of my eyes and disappear. Aunt Simran doesn't seem to notice, so I pretend not to either. 'Thank you,' I whisper. I should be excited to see Mum's room, but my feelings are fluttering all over the place.

'I'll be back in a minute.' Aunt Simran bustles off, leaving me staring dreamily at everything.

'You've come home at last.' A soft voice wakes me from my daydream. An old woman, wearing a white *salwaar kameez* with a grey woollen shawl draped over her shoulders, comes down the staircase, stretches out her arms and draws me to her, wraps me in the warmth of her shawl. She smells of cinnamon and hot milk.

I don't know what to say. This must be Nani . . . Mum's mum.

I start to put my hands together to repeat the greeting Dad taught me. '*Sat—*' I begin, but the words stay knotted and won't come out.

She squeezes me so hard I think I might pass out. 'Look at you,' she says, her eyes watery. 'So big now, but still the same eyes, same smile. You look just like . . .' She trails off, unable to say the name we both know is on her lips. *Chinty*. Mum's name.

I think of how evasive Aunt Simran was when I

asked about Mum in the car. *What happened here? Why won't they talk about her?*

Nani releases me, wrings her hands and looks away down the corridor. Aunt Simran stands at the top of the stairs and beckons to me. I lug my case up, resting it on each step, trying to be as careful as I can, before Aunt Simran takes it and shows me to a room on the right of the staircase. It's dark inside, but a small lamp on the bedside table sends out a cheerful light.

'It's too late to eat anything big now,' says Aunt Simran kindly. 'But try the warm milk and pastry, sleep well and I'll see you in the morning.' She closes the door gently and leaves me standing in the middle of the room, my head swimming. I feel light-headed and hold on to the table where the pastry and milk Aunt Simran mentioned are waiting. I take a tiny nibble but can't swallow it and the milk has a weird creamy smell. I spit the bite of pastry into a tissue and throw it in the bin.

Something taps against the window and that same piercing scream sounds again; this time it's closer, as if it's right outside. Shivers shoot up my spine as I kick my trainers off and jump into bed fully clothed. With my eyes shut tight I lie stiff, listening to the strange new sounds, wishing for morning to come soon. Slipping slowly into sleep I hear that song again – someone singing my name . . .

Tamarind.

The sun filters through the shutters, casting patterned light across the room, like golden dust floating in the air. A dream clings to my mind – a familiar tune and white blossom . . . but it's already slipping away. I expected it to be warm in India, but it's cold and I shiver, pulling the soft duvet tighter and snuggling further down the bed. Outside I can hear the clinking of plates and the hum of low voices, chairs being scraped against the floor and a shushing of leaves making sounds like the sea.

The thought that I'm in Mum's room relaxes me for a moment and I fall into a doze. I forget where I am and listen for the blare of the rush hour. But outside there are no trucks or buses; it's quiet except for an unfamiliar bird cry that reminds me I'm so far from home.

My throat begins to tighten again as I remember how everything is different now. It was Dad and me, the dream team, for so long, but life has changed so much since Chloe moved in. And I know I have to try harder but I miss it just being us. No more lazy Sundays, eating home-made pancakes in bed, watching TV together. We haven't done that in ages. Like Dad said, Chloe is part of the family now. But sometimes it feels like it isn't my family any more.

I get out of bed and look around. I don't see anything that could belong to Mum in here, but of course they probably put all her things away a long time ago. There are a few books up on the shelf above the bed and some of the titles are in English, but I'm too weary to think of reading right now.

There's another bed opposite mine and it's made up in the same flowery linen as the one I slept in last night. Tucked under the duvet is a battered teddy bear with one eye missing. On the bedside table are some tiny green bootees.

I pick them up, peering closely. They're slightly faded but look as if they've been treasured. Maybe they were mine when I was a baby, or Mum's.

I put the bootees back and go to the window, grab hold of the handles and try pulling it up. It's stiff, like it hasn't been opened for a while. After some tugging it flies up and the wind whistles through the slats. I part the shutters and they slide away either side of the window.

I gasp and take it all in.

The garden is in full sun. Mist rises from lawns bordered by short clipped hedges and roses droopy with raindrops. I can't tell where the garden ends, but I can see the top branches of a tree a way off, its base hidden by the garden, its feathery leaves shaking in the breeze as if they're whispering secrets. I wonder if that's Mum's tree, the one in the photo with the swing. 'I'm here, Mum,' I whisper.

I let the sun warm my face, amazed by the mountains beyond the garden, snow-peaked and majestic, rising into the morning sky. High up, birds with wide-stretched wings spiral slowly on the currents, calling as they fly.

I peer down at the mound that the house sits on, with its narrow terraces covered in blue dancing poppies. To one side of the house there's a walled orchard of fruit trees, dark plums pulling laden branches to the ground, rosy apples and even peaches, I think. Straining my eyes further round the orchard, I spy chickens scratching at the earth and a plump black cow grazing alongside them.

My eyes swivel back to the main garden and are drawn to its edges where the neat borders, with their swirls of rose bushes in deep shades of pink and crimson, end – to where the grass has been allowed to grow longer. The sloped roof of a little summer house peeks through the sunlight. I think I might explore this morning, get to know the place where

Mum grew up, and see if I can find out for myself the things nobody will tell me.

There's the scream again, the same as last night. High-pitched, sharp. Fear spikes through me and I slam the window down.

It can't be anything dangerous, I tell myself, not so near to the house. Aunt Simran said it was nothing.

Even so, I sit on the bed, try to stop my heart racing, count to five and focus on the room instead. It's really sweet, the sort of room you read about in stories. It's got golden monkeys painted in a line around the walls, and shelves crammed with books of all sizes. The stripped wooden floor has a thick red rug across it.

I walk over to a door and give it a gentle push – it's even got its own small bathroom! There's a cute little bath with fluffy towels piled on a shelf and blocks of lemon-scented soap.

I study the family photos sitting on a bright blue chest of drawers, some of them from long enough ago to be black and white. In one of them, the house is covered in snow, its balconies and verandah totally white. I gaze at the picture; it's the first time I've seen one of the whole building from the outside. I didn't have a clue from that corner on Mum's photo that it was going to be so *big*. Why didn't Dad tell me? It feels like he's been lying to me all my life . . . I don't know who he is *or* who *I* am any more.

There's a knock on the door and it suddenly flies open, bringing noises from the rest of the house bouncing into the room, someone running down the stairs, a voice that sounds like Aunt Simran getting things organized. I'm not sure why but I spring back into bed – oddly guilty about exploring the room. I can't help feeling like an intruder.

'You've been asleep ages.' It's Arjun. He struggles into the room carrying a wooden tray piled with tea things, which he practically drops on the table next to my bed – along with the doorknob. He catches me looking at it and sighs. 'This house is so old – things are always falling apart. Chacha Dev will fix it later.'

I pull a face. 'Sorry,' I say. 'Should I have got up early?'

'No, don't worry. We're allowed to lie in when we're here. It doesn't matter, we're on holiday.'

'So you don't usually live here?'

He pours me a cup of tea from the pot and pulls up a chair. 'No. We usually live in Rinigaar – you know, where the airport is. We've got a modern house there, that's where I go to school. This is the house that's been in our family for ever. Nanijee lives here all the time with Uma and Chacha Dev to

30

help . . . it's where my papa grew up.' He coughs. 'And your mum.'

I begin to get excited but try to control my voice. 'What else do you know about my mum?'

'I'm sorry, Tamarind.' He gives me a sad look. 'I don't know anything else.'

My heart falls with a crash.

'Oh, and I made this for you.' Arjun places a small, neatly folded origami bird on the bedcovers.

I try to hide my disappointment that he's changed the subject so quickly. 'It's amazing!' I admire the carefully made little bird, then peer at Arjun over the cup. He's got a friendly face and brown wavy hair that's a bit long and messy. I blow at the tea, the steam rising and warming my cheeks.

'I thought you'd be on that gamer thing,' I say, 'not bringing me breakfast in bed.'

'It doesn't work up here – no signal or wifi. That's how I got into origami – you have to find your own things to do. I can show you how to make one later if you want. And everyone has to help out here. Except *Princess* Sufia who only helps herself out.'

'Who's Princess Sufia?' I wonder if maybe she's a real princess. Living in this house, it wouldn't be too strange.

'My older sister. She's seventeen, four years

younger than Kamaal – she'll be arriving later.' Arjun rolls his eyes. Then he pauses. 'When you'd gone to bed Nanijee kept crying.' He bites his lip. 'She said she couldn't believe you were here at last.'

'I don't know why Dad never brought me before,' I say, looking around the room. 'I wanted us to come. But he's always been quiet about Mum.' *Just like everyone here*, I think.

Arjun looks away at the window and doesn't say anything.

I take a small sip of the tea. 'Oh!' I cry. 'It's spicy. I didn't expect that. We just have plain old English tea at home.'

Arjun smiles, obviously relieved I'm not going to ask him about Mum again. 'So was that your new ma, I mean *mum*, at the airport?'

'I just call her Chloe.' I try to sound like I don't care. 'She's been desperate for Dad to bring her to India.'

Arjun appears to sense how uncomfortable I am because he stands up awkwardly. 'Once you're ready, I'll show you around if you like.' He picks up the doorknob. 'And I'll get this sorted. See you downstairs.'

'Arjun,' I say, rubbing at the sleep still clinging to my eyes. 'Thank you for the tea.'

'That's OK. Nanijee said to tell you there's breakfast on the verandah. And by the way, my room's at the end of the corridor, just in case.' He pushes the door behind him, leaving it slightly open.

I check my phone but there are no messages: only Rafi's last one and my reply that pinged back – and, just as Arjun promised, there's no signal either. Once again that lonely feeling falls like ice under my skin.

5

I dress slowly, throwing aside all the shorts I brought, certain it was going to be hot despite Dad's warnings, and choose jeans and a thick sweatshirt. As I open the door on to the landing, my stomach tightens and I begin to feel all alone again.

The sound of chattering voices tinkles up the wide stairs that smell of old-fashioned polish. If Rafi was here, we'd slide down the banisters together and end up in a bundle of laughter at the bottom. But she's not, so I walk carefully down each creaking step until I'm in the hallway with its vast paintings of bewildered-looking animals.

'Out here,' calls Aunt Simran.

I follow the chatter through a large dining room where French doors lead on to the verandah. Arjun is already there, tucking into a square of crispy flatbread, smothered in butter.

It's sunny but a chill wind lifts the tablecloth. Nani looks out across the borders of pink and crimson roses and bushes of wide purple flowers towards the mountains beyond. 'Morning, Tamarind. Sorry for the weather. It looks like it's changing, storms coming – mountain storms. I hope it holds for a while so you can enjoy being outdoors, though.'

Kamaal is wearing headphones and tapping his fork in time to the music only *he* can hear. He looks up, slides the headphones off his right ear as he sees me. 'Hey, cuz,' he smiles. 'How was your first night in the mountains?'

'Good, thanks.'

'Cool.' He pops the headphones on, already back in his own world and tapping his fork again.

I shuffle round the table and find an empty seat beside Arjun, laid ready for breakfast. But when I begin to sit down, Nani frowns and Aunt Simran brings me towards her.

'Not there.'

The chair looks special, different to the rest, covered with turquoise blue velvet and sequins stitched to the fabric. I look at Arjun, but he stares at his plate and carries on stuffing bread into his mouth.

Aunt Simran clears her throat and looks at Nani.

'We . . . don't sit there.' She pats the bench beside her. 'Come. We want to know all about you, no need to be shy with family. What's your house like? And what do you like doing?'

I breathe out slowly, feel the heat rise. 'It's a bit boring compared to all this,' I begin, staring at the garden bursting with so many flowers and clipped bushes it looks more like a park. 'Not much to tell really. I've lived in Bristol with Dad in the same small house' – I want to say a normal house – 'since I was little. Just me and him until . . .' I trail off, start again. 'Until they got married and Chloe moved in too . . . Granny and Grandpa, Dad's parents, live round the corner but I don't have any other family. I started secondary school this year, I like playing football and drawing.' I really want to tell them that I usually only eat plain food and definitely no chilli, but how can I tell them that? Ever since I mistook a green chilli for a French bean I'm totally paranoid.

My mouth has gone dry with all the attention. I notice a small woman with crinkled skin, wearing a green sari and carrying a huge tray of crispy white pancakes, has appeared in the doorway.

The pancakes are folded in half and stuffed with yellow cubes of something. A strong smell of fried ginger wafts towards me and I squint to check for the red-hot slices of chilli that I fear are hidden inside. Dad said he warned them, didn't he? If this is breakfast, I know I won't be able to eat it; my stomach is stabbing already.

Suddenly I notice the woman carrying the tray is staring at me as though I've got two heads. Wedging the tray on to the table, she rushes over and grasps hold of my hands, stares into my eyes. I'm a bit freaked out because she's got a really firm grip and she's not letting go. 'Just like her ma,' she says, pressing my hands more tightly.

'Thank you, Uma,' says Aunt Simran firmly. 'Uma is our cook, Tamarind. She's been with the family for decades.'

Uma drops my hands and starts to leave the room. 'Come to see me in the kitchen, I'll make you some *gulab jaman* . . . Chinty loved my *gulab jaman*.'

Chinty? I'm longing to follow Uma into the kitchen, maybe even try the food she mentioned and ask her about my mum, but she's disappeared back into the house and Nani is coming round to my side of the table.

'Tamarind, *beta*, come,' says Nani. She clasps her soft hands around my face and lifts it towards her, kissing my cheeks. 'Did we make enough food for you? It is a celebration . . . at last you are here.' She pours an iced white drink into a steel tumbler. '*Lassi* . . . fresh from the cows.'

I stare at the shining tumbler, my throat tightening. *It's only milk, Tamarind – stop being so silly about it, how bad can it be?* All eyes are on me as I put the cold tumbler to my lips and take a sip of the iced drink. 'Yeuch.' I spit it out, without meaning to. 'It's salty!' I wipe my mouth and feel myself turn scarlet.

Both Arjun and Kamaal stare at their plates, their lips curling into small smiles.

Nani grabs a napkin and dabs at my mouth. Aunt Simran rushes to mop up the mess on the table.

'Sorry, Tamarind,' says Aunt Simran. 'I should have told you it was not a sweet smoothie like you are probably used to. *Lassi* is salty, darling. Don't worry – your papa sent us a little list in his letter so we won't let you starve. Uma can make you something you like.'

'It doesn't matter,' says Nani, continuing to dab the tablecloth even though she doesn't need to. 'Different place, different tastes . . . you'll get used to it.'

6

After some plain buttered toast and a mug of warm hot chocolate, me and Arjun head outside to kick a football about while all the grown-ups are busy. Kamaal is driving Aunt Simran to the village for supplies, Nani is settling down for a nap and Chacha Dev is fixing the doorknob on my bedroom door. In the enormous garden, we feel completely alone.

I dribble the ball on to the short grass and run circles around Arjun before passing to him. It's a relief to be doing something familiar.

'I play a bit of football,' he says. 'Only in the play-ground, though. Not like you. You are *fast*.' He chases after the ball – which has bounced off towards the house – and when he comes back, he slumps down on the grass to catch his breath, holding the ball between his feet. 'How did you get so good?'

I sit down beside him. 'I got into it because my best friend Rafi was mad for it. And then Mrs Wallis, our teacher at Primary, said it wasn't only boys that could play football and she persuaded us all to train, *really* hard. We set up a girls' team and got good, me and Rafi went to County level. That's quite high up.'

'You look like the professionals.' Arjun stops and suddenly bursts into giggles. 'I'm sorry, no offence but it was quite funny when you spat the *lassi* out everywhere.'

I don't know what to think at first but then I start to laugh too, all the tight coils of stress bursting out of me. 'Let's hope we don't get *lassi* for dinner too,' I say when we've both finally stopped laughing. 'To be honest, I usually just like plain food. Dad teases me about it.'

Arjun raises his eyebrows. 'Plain food . . . like what? Rice?'

'Rice is OK. Bread. Fish fingers.' I shrug.

'So you won't be up for the chilli challenge?'

'What's the chilli challenge?'

'It's when you get a plate of chillies and you don't know which ones are hot, really hot or basically going to kill you, and then you choose one and take a bite.'

My face must be turning pale because Arjun

quickly adds, 'It's only for fun and it's only usually me, Dad and Kamaal that do it.'

The thought of it makes my stomach clench with nerves. 'Maybe not just yet,' I say, meaning *definitely NEVER!*

There's a small silence, then Arjun scrambles up, says 'Watch this!' and kicks the ball – but instead of sliding between the terracotta pots we marked as goalposts, it's completely mis-aimed. Arjun groans as the ball rolls off to the edge of the neat garden.

I take pity. 'Don't worry – I'll get it!' I say, running after it. I peer through the long grass . . . we must be near the summer house I spotted from the bedroom window earlier. I spy the ball a metre or so in front of me and take a step into the tall grass. The world feels silent and still and some instinct compels me to stop – it's like a spell. I shut my eyes, feel the grass tickling my legs. Can I hear music on the wind?

'*Tamarind,*' I hear. A sing-song voice, soft as a whisper.

I turn round but Arjun is still way off, closer to the house. Besides, the voice emerged from beyond the long grass, as if someone out there was singing my name.

I'm about to go further but Arjun catches up with me.

'Is there a summer house?' I ask him, glancing through the sunlit grass in the direction of the voice.

'Yeah, it's in the wild bit of the garden over there. It's not really a summer house, just a sort of small hut. We don't have a gardener like we used to, only Chacha Dev, Uma's husband, so that part's like a jungle.'

'Could someone be in there?' I'm on the point of asking him about the singing.

But he's shaking his head. 'No way. It's out of bounds. Definitely don't go there. Nanijee will be really cross and get all upset again.'

'But why?'

'I don't know, but I *do* know that Nanijee is sensitive about some things and the hut is one of them.'

I frown. 'I really thought I heard something.'

Arjun shrugs. 'Probably an animal. We have all sorts living here. Deer, wildcats, snakes, all sorts of birds and sometimes bigger animals come down from the mountains, like bears, tigers and wolves. But don't worry, they tend to come at night if at all – when it's quiet.'

My eyes widen – and I listen more sharply, because whatever I heard through there, it definitely wasn't an animal.

'Come on – let's go. Nani will be anxious if she

sees us so close to the hut.'

I want to ignore Arjun and go through the long grass towards the small building. It feels like it's calling me. A tingle shoots up my spine as I see a movement flash through the long grass nearby, a swish of a golden tail . . . a wildcat maybe?

'Come on,' says Arjun, picking up the ball. 'Let's go back.'

When I wake up from the nap Nani insisted I had, I sleepily check my watch. I can't believe it's four o'clock and I still feel tired. I prop myself up against the headboard. I frown at my duvet: there are white petals scattered across the bed.

Has someone been in here while I've been asleep? I can't imagine Arjun doing that, or even Nani or Aunt Simran, and they couldn't have blown in; the windows and shutters are closed.

As I get out my clothes, I feel like there are hidden eyes watching me. Fear creeps from my toes to my stomach where it sits like a tiger, ready to pounce.

The red rug is sprinkled with something like glitter, but when I touch it with my fingertips it's more like dust, fine sandy dust. In a panic I hurry to dress and push the door open, flying down the stairs to the comfort of the family.

Along the dining table, sunbeams glint against the glasses, sending rainbows dancing across the green tiles of the verandah floor. The table is decorated with tea lights ready to be lit and fresh food is laid out along the centre.

I slide on to the bench beside Arjun, avoiding the mystery chair completely, the one no one is meant to sit at. It's carved from dark wood and looks almost like a throne with sturdy armrests; the turquoise velvet shines with tiny sequins. It looks like a special chair. Maybe this is where *Princess* Sufia sits.

Nani settles on the other side and takes my hand, stroking it softly, then starts singing to me. I'm not sure what to do so I let her carry on.

'All these years, Tamarind,' she says, when the song is finished, 'all these years you don't come home but now you're here.' She drapes the shawl over her shoulder, dabbing at her eyes with a corner. She lifts a plate, piling it with yellow rice, almonds and yoghurt. 'You like lamb *kofta*?'

'I don't eat meat, Nani. I'm a vegetarian, so no thank you.'

'Oh dear . . . yes, I remember.' She gets up and calls into the kitchen. 'Uma, please bring the *dahl* dumplings for Tamarind.'

'Honestly, I'm fine with the rice.' I spoon a tiny

mouthful. 'It's really yummy.'

Nani sits back down and begins feeding me the rice. I feel stupid, like I'm about two, but she seems really happy so I open my mouth like a baby bird and let her carry on. I must have been tiny when Nani last saw me – maybe she fed me my milk just like this?

I hear the faint sound of a car scrunching along gravel and wonder if they have someone coming for dinner.

A tall girl appears from the garden, followed by Kamaal. She calls out before I can see her properly, 'I'm home!' Her high ponytail swings from side to side as she strides on to the verandah and throws her bag down. 'I didn't know we were having guests,' she says, staring at me. 'And why is Nanijee feeding her like a baby?' she snorts.

7

The girl carries on staring at me but I focus on my plate instead, sneak a look at her from under my lashes. The sides of her hair are shaved short and now that she's standing in the light I can see that the tip of her ponytail is dyed pink. She looks really cool, and I think she knows it.

Kamaal sits down noisily and begins helping himself to food.

'Sufia,' says Nani, continuing to feed me. 'This is not a guest, this is cousin Tamarind – she's come home. Remember?'

'Oh!' She sounds annoyed. 'You know I don't always bother to read the whole of Mum's letters.' She darts me a shrivelling look. 'I hope you're not staying too long?'

My chest tightens and I feel the food rising back up. Just as I was starting to feel at home I'm slammed right back to being the outsider again.

'Shh . . .' says Aunt Simran. 'She stays as long as she wishes.'

'Don't take any notice,' says Arjun to me, under his breath. 'Sufia's been away at school and she's always like this when she gets back.'

Sufia folds her arms.

'I put Tamarind in your room,' says Aunt Simran, 'so you can catch up and make friends. Now take your bags up and then come and eat.'

Sufia scowls at me. 'Make friends? I'd rather sleep in the attic room.'

'In.' Aunt Simran pushes her towards the house and follows her inside.

'She is silly,' says Nani, patting my back. 'In this house there's plenty of rooms for everyone but Simran's right – it's nice for you girls to share. Here, have more rice.'

I can barely get my words out. 'No more, please.' I wish I hadn't come and I really don't want to cry.

Inside, Aunt Simran and Sufia are arguing. 'But I thought Nanijee said she never wanted to see him again.' Sufia's making no effort to keep her voice down. Her words shoot on to the verandah like poisonous arrows. 'He ruined this whole family! And she—' Aunt Simran cuts her off.

'That's enough, Sufia.'

He . . . was she talking about Dad? Why do they all hate him so much? Why won't anyone tell me what's going on?

I grip the edge of the table and think I might throw up. I feel totally homesick and if only I could get a signal on that stupid phone Dad gave me, I'd ring him right now and tell him to come back and get me . . . except I'd be in the way there as well.

'It's not Tamarind's fault.' It's Aunt Simran's voice now. 'You *will* make her welcome, Sufia, despite everything that's happened. Now go to your room.'

Nani's staring into the garden and Arjun's squirming in his seat, looking everywhere except at me.

Uma comes out with a steaming bowl of lentil dumplings. She puts it in front of me. 'Chinty loved these. I hope you will too.'

But I stand up and push past Arjun, not caring if I'm being rude, and run away from the house into the garden, stumbling down the steps.

Nani's voice trails after me. 'Tamarind, *beta* . . . come back.'

I keep running, not knowing where I'm headed, everything blurry, feeling more out of place than I've ever felt before. I sprint across the lawns, scraping past bushes prickly with thorns, desperate to get as

48

far away from *her* as possible.

I'm not going back to the house and I'm never speaking to Sufia. Does she think I wanted to come here in the first place?

My heart keeps thumping, my chest aching, and confused, angry tears steam down my cheeks. How could Dad do this to me? He's left me with people I don't know, who seem to hate him, and he didn't even tell me why.

I storm away, even further into the garden, where it turns wilder and overgrown, where no one will find me and I can hide from them all. Blood drums loudly in my ears as I push through tall grasses and stinging nettles as high as my waist and stumble out the other side.

The light is fading and I can't see the ground clearly in the long shadows. My foot catches on a rock, sending me tumbling and I let out a cry as I land heavily on the grass with a smack, my palms stinging.

Arjun said there were snakes in this wild part of the garden and I quickly lift my head, standing up shakily. Before me looms a row of slender trees, a copse. I brush the mud from my clothes and step closer; their bark is papery white, the dark leaves rustling in the wind, making a ghostly shushing sound.

Peering between the spaces in the trees where the evening shadows are beginning to appear, I notice the outline of an old wooden hut, its sloped roof covered in tangles of dense ivy. It's the summer house that I spied from my bedroom window, the one Arjun told me is forbidden – but what do I care now? I feel a strong pull towards the hut, remembering the strange song I heard earlier.

The small square windows are strung with cobwebs and the panels of the shed bleached silver from wind and rain. I rub at a dirty pane of glass and put my eye close. There are things inside but I can't make them out. I find the door and rattle the handle but it's locked and won't open.

I hunt around the doorway; perhaps there's a key somewhere, but I don't find anything. Around the side of the hut there's a big plant pot with an over-grown bush in it. That's just the sort of place you'd find a hidden key. I stick my hand into the soil and fish about, but there's nothing there.

As I kick at the ground in frustration, my eyes catch a patch of loose grass, piled into a pyramid shape. When I knock the grass away with my foot, the soil underneath looks like it's been recently raked. I bend low on hands and knees, easily dig my fingers into the ground and feel cold metal buried about a fist-length in the earth. I wrap my fingers around it and bring out an old brass key.

My heart pumps as I hurriedly slot it into the lock and twist to the left. It turns easily, like it's used to being opened. Placing my palms flat against the door I push slowly and step inside the hut.

8

It's dark and gloomy and smells musty and resinous, as if I'm right inside the heart of a tree.

Once my eyes get used to the lack of light, I see a set of bunks on either side carved from old knotted wood. Each bed is made up with pretty patterned duvets, piles of cushions carefully placed on top. Although it looked abandoned on the outside, someone's clearly been looking after the inside of the hut. A brass candle-holder is screwed to the wall beside each bed with a half-burnt candle in one of them.

I sit down on one of the beds and notice that there are some faint letters scratched on to the headboard. I run my finger over them: C-h-i-n-t-y – *Chinty*! Mum must have played in here . . . she must have slept in this little bed. My head spins and I lean back on the headboard, bright colours swirling across my eyelids. I hear that song again, calling me with its soft, lilting voice – *Tamarind*.

I shake myself back and open my eyes, search the drawer of the bedside table and find a box of matches to light the candle on the wall. The yellow flame sends long black shadows flitting around the hut. I sit down on the bed again – my mum's bed.

I keep thinking about what's just happened. I'm not sure why Sufia was so mean to me, but it's something to do with my dad. It was odd the way Aunt Simran wasn't exactly friendly to Dad at the airport, but nobody apart from Sufia is saying anything and I don't know why they're so angry with him. There are so many unanswered questions and I don't know who to ask.

The door opens a crack and I wonder if maybe it's Sufia come to have a proper go at me, face to face . . . or is it something much more dangerous? There's a piercing scream, like the one I heard when I arrived but closer this time, and I remember Arjun saying bigger animals can descend here from the mountains. I jump up, shrink back from the door, into the corner of the bed. This time, the scream was loud and very close. My body begins to tremble. It could be a wild Himalayan tiger out hunting its prey. I glance around the hut but there's nowhere for me to run so I throw the covers over my head and curl into a tiny ball.

My heart pounds frantically as the door creaks a bit more and weird spooky shapes project across the light filtering through the blanket. The door flings open and footsteps pad closer. The bed dips down beside me. Whatever it is, it's right next to me now. My heart is racing . . . and then – weirdly – it's pulling the blanket from over my head. I blink.

It's a monkey! It's *only* a monkey! That's what has been screaming in the garden all this time. Relief floods me and I examine the creature more closely. He's covered in honey-coloured fur, parts of it turning grey. He reaches out and strokes my hair and I'm not sure what to do so I sit there stiffly. He takes my face in his smooth palms and gives me a sorrowful look with his huge dark eyes.

He hobbles off the bed and disappears underneath it. I've never been this close to a monkey – I've only ever seen them behind plastic screens at the zoo – and I'm feeling a bit nervous, but after everything that's happened I wouldn't mind making friends with him.

I lie flat on the floor, press myself into the smooth floorboards and try to entice him out. Two bright eyes blink at me in the darkness.

I push my arm under the bed. 'Here, little fella,' I say, pretending I've got something tasty in my hand. 'Come on, I won't bite.' It would be so nice to stroke his soft fur.

He stays under the bed and won't come out, so I wriggle under as well. 'Come on, you silly monkey.' He's right up against the wall, so I push on my elbows, moving closer to him.

Even though it's dark down here I can see that the monkey is pulling on a loose floorboard. He wedges his fingers under a section and yanks at it. Then he scuttles to one side, tugging at my sleeve.

I strain my eyes, peering into the gap where the piece of floorboard has been removed, but it's no good, it's just too dark. I shuffle backwards, brushing the floor with my stomach. If I can get the candle off the holder I'll be able to shine the light down there and see what it is.

The monkey climbs on to the bed and watches me as I wiggle the candle free, clapping his hands.

Back on my stomach, I push the candle ahead of me until it's just on the edge of the gap, and shift the floorboard to get a better look. The monkey crouches beside me, peering underneath too. I can make out a box inside the space under the floor and dip my hand in. I'm just about to lift it out when I hear footsteps outside and I quickly drop it back into the gap.

I squeeze out from under the bed and can't see the monkey anywhere. I dart my eyes towards the open door and spot the very end of a long honey-coloured tail and what looks like a trail of sparkling gold dust following it.

Gold dust? I feel a twitch tickle up my spine and I'm frozen to the spot. I'm probably just imagining things: the candlelight casts a strange glow in here.

The door opens and it's Arjun. He's out of breath; he clearly ran here. 'What are you doing?' he yells. 'I *told* you we're not allowed in the hut.'

'But why not? This was where my mum used to come and play, isn't it?'

Arjun shifts around, looks away towards the open door.

'I *know* it is,' I say, more sharply than I meant to. 'I've seen where she scratched her name on the headboard. Why won't anyone speak about my mum? *Why* would Nani be upset? *Why* shouldn't I be here?' I'm desperate now and step towards him. '*Please*, Arjun, tell me.'

His cheeks turn red. 'My *babajee* built the hut for my dad and your mum when they were little, and now everyone is banned. I don't know why. I get that you want to find out about your mum, but stop asking me. I'm not the one who knows.'

I lean against the wall and try to calm down. 'Y . . . you won't tell them I was here, will you?'

'No, I won't tell. Promise. And Sufia has been grounded.'

My throat is dry and my voice comes out all croaky. 'Thank you.'

I don't know if I should tell Arjun about the box under the floorboards or about the monkey. I decide not to. He was upset enough that I was here – he won't like it if he knows I was poking around. Maybe he'd tell the rest of the family. Arjun seems nice, but I haven't known him long – he's not exactly my friend.

If I can find a torch in the house I'll come back later, I decide, at night when everyone's asleep.

9

I squint at my watch under the darkness of my bedcovers. The electric-blue numbers read just past midnight and I begin to creep out of bed. I know it's out of bounds but I don't care. I slept like the dead last night – jet lag catching me up, I suppose – and a whole day has gone by, just trying so hard to be polite to everyone, and out with Arjun kicking a ball round the garden again, while Sufia seems to be doing her best to avoid me or throws hate-eyes my way. Every now and then I catch a faint glimpse of a golden tail too. So I'm extra-determined to go back to the hut tonight and find out what's under that floorboard.

I grab the torch I found in the side-table drawer, lace up my black trainers with a blue tick along the side, and click open the door to the landing. Everything is quiet, the glow from the lamps in the hallway spinning black shadows up the walls.

I shoot a swift glance upwards, to the next flight of stairs where Sufia's sleeping, swallow my nerves and hurry down.

My heart stammers. What would they say if they caught me out of bed so late? Shining the torch ahead of me, I tiptoe along the cold floor of the hallway. As quickly as I can, I find my way out through the dining room, on to the verandah. A flame of excitement burning my chest, I rush down the wooden steps, brushing past the poppies shifting in the wind and enter the beckoning coolness of the garden.

The darkness takes me by surprise. I'm used to streetlights, not this overwhelming sky with its trillions of stars. The torch hardly seems to make a difference as I pick my way along the wet lawn, zigzagging towards the hut.

A dank, earthy smell rises through the gloom as I wade through the too tall grass and can't help imagining something stalking me, a wild bear about to pounce through the darkness, claws sharpened ready to grab me from behind. A far-off howling noise makes my blood pump harder, faster.

It's different from the screaming sound I've been hearing, that I now know is from the monkey. No: this sounds like *wolves*. I think back to what Arjun told me, that they sometimes venture down into the garden. *And* I'm pretty sure they can eat people. Maybe I should turn back!

I glance over my shoulder, but the house is too far away now. I gather my courage, tell myself not to be such a coward and keep stepping into the halo of weak light cast by the torch. Tramping through the final nettles, I raise my hands high to avoid their sting and remember the rock that tripped me up last time, and find it with the light.

As I step through the copse lit white by the moon, I know I'm nearly there, but keep my breath squashed tight, my fists wrapped hard around the torch, and search for the key in the ground where I found it before and hid it after I left.

Once inside, everything is just as before, spookily quiet. I collapse on to my stomach, pointing the torch under the bed, and wriggle towards the gap in the floorboards. Balancing the torch on the floor beside me, I gently lift the box out and push it to where I can take a better look.

It's only a long cardboard box, but it's been covered in pretty paper and across the top there are cut-out letters that read: *Chinty's Secret Box* . . . And underneath, in red pen: *keep out!!!!*

My heart pounds as I open the lid. Surely Mum

wouldn't mind *me* looking into her secret box?

The first thing I see inside is an arrow. I lift it out and examine it. The tip is made from a beaten piece of metal and the wooden shaft is painted gold, the white feather fletching on the end covered in gold glitter. It has a home-made look to it. There's a small box of face paints in there too. I open the lid and sniff them, wet my finger on my tongue and prod it into the silver block. Although it's dried out, I still feel the gritty paint on my fingertip, imagine Mum dressing up, decorating her face with this same paint. I smear it across my cheeks and smile.

The final thing is a small blue box right in the corner. I open it carefully, slowly, instinctively knowing that whatever is inside must be really special. There's folded red tissue paper inside, and when I unwrap it I discover the most beautiful ring. I hold it carefully between my shaking fingers and look at it closely. In its centre is a bright green stone, about the size of a five-pence piece, surrounded by a silver eight-pointed star.

Bubbles of excitement make my heart beat faster. At last I've got something of Mum's, something precious, special. I feel so close to her, as if she's right here beside me in this hut: it's the strangest, warmest feeling.

The stone is crafted like a proper jewel with small chips carved into it. When I shine the torch on it, each intricate face glitters. When I slip it on to my middle finger it fits perfectly. I hold it up to the window and the ring glows, sending a beam of light into the room as the starlight hits it. I gasp, remembering the trail of gold dust that followed the monkey, and feel a little light-headed, just like I did before. I blink. It's not surprising I'm seeing and hearing things, I've not eaten very much since I got here and the time difference is confusing me. I'm sure it's just jet lag. Sure enough, as I move the ring away from the window, the glow fades. There's that voice again . . . far off somewhere, singing through the trees . . .

Tamarind.

Why do I keep hearing it – or am I just imagining it?

I hear footsteps smacking against the grass outside and freeze. Who else can be awake at this time? I hurriedly shove everything back in the box and manage to push it under the bed, but keep the ring on my finger, clasping my hands tightly behind my back.

The door cracks open, startling me. It's Sufia.

'What are you doing here?' she says, sounding as surprised as me.

'Nothing . . . I mean, I couldn't sleep and came to get some fresh air.'

'No one's allowed in here, you know . . . especially *you*.' She narrows her eyes into slits. 'If Nanijee knew you'd been in here without her permission, she'd go nuts.'

I wonder if I should say that Arjun had been here yesterday as well, but I guess that's not going to make a difference and would probably get him into all sorts of trouble.

Wearing Mum's ring is making me braver and I stand tall. '*You* come here though, don't you? Some-one's been taking care of this place, even though it's forbidden.'

'That's none of your business,' she says, shifting closer. 'Anyway . . . why are you snooping around?'

'I'm n-not snooping.' My throat feels dry and my voice comes out in a squeak.

'I'd say coming into someone else's house and then prying where you shouldn't be is definitely snooping *and* I've been grounded because of you.'

'It's not my fault.'

'Well, I'd say it definitely *is* your fault. There isn't anyone else you can blame it on, is there?' She's glaring at me, and even in this dim light I can see she's really angry. 'And the sooner you're gone the better!' She spits the words out like the worst taste ever. 'What's that behind your back?' Sufia circles me, as if she's a wolf stalking a wounded animal. I snap my hands to the front, folding them across my chest, hiding the ring. She's way taller than me and peers down. I try to hold myself tall but my stomach clenches as she faces me and yanks my hands out.

She stares at my finger, at the ring. 'What's that?' Before I have time to react or stop her, she grabs my hand and forces the ring off my finger, holding it high above her head. 'It's Auntie Chinty's ring,' she says, her eyes widening, as if she's speaking to herself. 'The one from the old photos – she wore it every-where when she was young.' She clenches her jaw harder. 'Where did you get it?'

It's as if wearing the ring has woken something inside me, a power I didn't know I had. I feel stronger than before. Just when I think I'm about to crumble to dust, my spirit rises like a mythological bird spreading its wings. 'Don't shout at me,' I say, in a quiet, determined voice. 'I have every bit of right to be here as you do.' I try to keep my voice from quivering. 'Everyone has welcomed me, apart from you, but it doesn't matter. I was born here and it's my home too . . . my mum would have wanted me to see it, I know she would.' I falter, swallowing to control myself. 'And she would have wanted me to have her ring – so give it back.' I hold out my hand.

Sufia is silent, but her cheeks are red and strangely she looks like she might cry. 'No.' She clutches it tightly, holding it firmly to her chest.

Without thinking, I launch into her, snatching at it, trying to prise it away. But she lifts it even higher.

'Can't get it now, can you?' She glares at me, her eyes sparkling with fury. 'You don't know the first thing about your mum and you never will.'

Sufia slips the ring into her pocket and grabs me by the shoulders. Her fingernails pinch my skin as she shoves me out of the hut.

10

I storm away from the hut, Sufia's words slicing into me like a knife, but I won't look round. I just keep walking straight ahead, shoulders back. Tears spill down my cheeks and fall in huge drops to the ground. She's right: I don't know *anything* about my mum and just when I'd found something that belonged to her, something special, *that's* been snatched away from me too.

I wipe away my tears as I reach the house – but when I gaze up at the verandah and my bedroom window, I suddenly don't want to go inside. Instead, I raise my eyes to the stars and try to hold on to the feeling I had when I wore Mum's ring, like a spark of knowledge that it was all meant to be, that I was meant to come here, that I belong.

A thought keeps prickling the back of my mind and it won't go away. What if the beam of light from the ring was leading me somewhere? It was so strong and so bright when I held it up to the window – brighter than a torch beam. What if it's not all just tiredness and jet lag? What if there really is something like magic in this place? If Sufia hadn't interrupted me I would have found out more . . . but now she's taken it.

Thoughts whirlpool around my mind and I know there's no way I could fall asleep. I sit on the damp lawn and listen to the night sounds of the garden – insects clicking and whirring, leaves rustling, owls hooting. After a while, I hear a familiar screaming noise behind me – quite near.

I sit up, my eyes widening as I notice a monkey sitting on the grass nearby. It's definitely the strange golden monkey I saw in the hut before: I can tell by the silver in his fur. When he moves, shifting closer towards me, it's like he's got a halo of gold dust all around him, his fur standing out against the darkness of the night. I really *didn't* imagine it before.

He stands and leaps away through the garden, towards the wild bit, before hesitating, glancing back at me. He wants me to follow him.

But how can I go, after what Arjun said about the dangers lurking out here? I gaze at the indigo night beyond the lawn, worry churning my stomach at what could be hidden there.

The monkey runs back to me and impatiently opens his mouth to make that awful screaming noise.

'Shhh,' I whisper, glancing up at the house, and he stops. Does he really understand me?

I zip my warm jumper up to the top, glad I thought to wear it earlier, and keep my hand clasped around the torch in the pocket. Suddenly I don't care about the danger: I need answers and I know I won't find them unless I follow him.

The monkey takes my hand and leads me past the hut – where I step quietly, afraid of attracting Sufia's attention – deeper and deeper into the wild garden. Where is he taking me? Suddenly he drops my hand, gives one of his high-pitched screams and sprints ahead.

'Wait, come back! Don't leave me in the dark,' I hiss. I run after him, chasing through the high grass. I shine the torch into the dark, trying to catch a glimpse of the monkey's gold fur – I see him! I run faster, my breath ragged, feet pounding the ground. It feels good – clean air burning my lungs. I want the smoky blue night to swallow me whole.

I keep going, further away from the hut and the house, stumbling into brambles sharp with thorns that tear at my skin. Suddenly running doesn't feel so good any more. How big are these gardens? They seem to go on for ever.

Picking through the patch of brambles forces me to slow down and I pause to catch my breath. Sufia's probably trying on Mum's ring – I imagine it now, swallowing the lump in my throat. Tomorrow, I'm determined I'll get the ring back.

The wind shakes the leaves of the trees and they rustle as if they're breathing secrets. I peer ahead, trying to work out which way the monkey went, and shine the torch into a blanket of ghostly mist, which drops around me like a cloak. I trip forwards, arms straight ahead trying to feel for something to anchor me, but there's nothing to grab hold of. The ground feels soft, almost wet, and my feet squelch and slip below me.

I feel a tugging on my sleeve and when I look down there's a tiny hand wrapped around my fingers.

'Hello again!' I let out the tight breath at last. 'I thought I'd lost you.'

He seems tired and slowly pulls me along through the thinning mist, making high-pitched chattering noises. When I glance down I see the arc of impossible gold dust as he flicks his tail through the night air.

I let the monkey lead me further into the under-growth, further into the unknown.

Black shadowy tree limbs appear on either side, spreading their branches low. The monkey and I walk hand in hand through the milky darkness where a white owl crosses our path, shuddering its wings, making my heart rap harder.

'I'm glad you're here,' I tell him, clutching his hand more tightly. 'But where are you taking me? Are we even in the garden any more?'

He gives me a little monkey grin and squeezes my hand back.

The sky above us brightens and a full moon spreads jagged shadows across the snow-capped mountains in the distance.

There in front of me, lit up by moonbeams, is a crumbling stone archway smothered in spiralling plants, the entrance to a neglected part of the garden. On top of the arch is a worn statue of a majestic-looking woman, standing tall with vast wings behind her. To either side sit two stone owls. Her feet are talons and she rests them lightly on two lions who lie beneath her. One hand is raised as if she's beckoning me forward.

Suddenly the monkey chatters and disappears into the trees.

Sweat beads across my forehead. Where am I? I need to turn back – this is stupid. I can't even see the house any more. There are wolves out here – maybe other things too. An icy wind lifts the leaves gathered at the foot of the archway, swirls them until they lift off the ground and rise to the top, falling through the air like dark snow.

An echoing giggle from behind me makes me jump and I hear the tune I heard when I arrived, but the humming, lilting voice is closer this time, closer and closer . . .

11

The song stops and the silence, somehow, is even more unnerving.

'Who's there?' I spin round, trying to stop my heart from pattering. I can't see anybody. But I definitely heard *something*. I think it's the song, the melody from the first night and the one I keep dreaming and hearing all around me. 'Is . . . is there somebody out there?'

I glance over my shoulder again but everything has been gobbled up by the night, while ahead of me the archway is filled with a shaft of silver moonlight. Did I imagine it? I start to walk forward.

But then a musical voice comes again, and this time it's not singing: '*Hurry up . . .*' The trilling voice is right behind me now and it stops me dead in my tracks. Butterflies begin fizzing through my stomach – like something exciting and maybe nerve-wracking is about to happen. That's it: I'm not waiting for whoever – *whatever* – it is to jump out at me! I run under the archway, veering to the left, sliding about on fallen leaves until I'm heaving for breath.

I don't need the torch any more – the moon is like a huge spotlight illuminating the overgrown garden, full of tangled paths. Scratching sounds in the undergrowth make me dart behind a decaying wooden structure overloaded with scented flowers, their drowsy smell reaching my nose, almost making me swoon. I hold myself steady and look around, searching for whoever's following me, listening for their footsteps.

Arjun warned me to keep away from here; he told me it was dangerous and now it's too late.

I hear the high sing-song voice again. '*Race you to the swing.*' My heart stammers and I'm about to stumble backwards but an icy hand grabs mine. I startle, terror flooding me. 'Careful . . . what's wrong?' A smiling face appears through the darkness. A girl, about my age. 'I was getting *sooo* tired waiting.' She wraps her arms around me and gives me the biggest hug ever.

I wriggle away from her, feeling confused and still half afraid, but she slings an arm across my shoulder. 'I'm so glad you're back,' she says, as if we're long-lost friends. Who is this girl and what is she doing in the family garden?

I can't stop staring. She's just a bit taller than me and her long plaits are twisted across the top of her head. She's wearing an embroidered flowery dress with loose trousers underneath, and a thick sheepskin waistcoat over the top, with a dagger in a leather sheath slung around her hips. I've never seen anyone dressed like *this* before.

She curls her arm into mine and before I can ask any questions, she starts running, dragging me alongside. 'Slow down,' I say, my breath rattling out of me. 'Who *are* you?'

I hear a scream and the monkey appears from nowhere, his gold dust shimmering the night.

'Hanu,' she laughs. 'There you are, naughty monkey.'

He runs to her and she lifts him up awkwardly, struggling to hold him. 'You're too big for this now,' she says affectionately.

'So he's *your* monkey?'

'Yes,' she says happily. 'You're mine, aren't you, little Hanu?'

He gives us both a cheeky grin as the girl takes my hand again and together the three of us chase through the garden, the girl tugging me onwards.

We seem to have done a big loop of the wild garden, ducking under trees, kicking through fallen leaves and twigs until I just make out the house again in the far-off distance, its twinkling lights peeping through the darkness.

We shoot backwards and forwards, round tree trunks and spiralling paths, and finally stop at the tree I saw from my window. There's a rope swing hooked on to the branch, just like the one in Mum's photo. I stand beneath the enormous tree, its branches spreading like a canopy above me, the green feathery leaves waving in the breeze. *Mum was here*, I think. I press my palms against its thick bark, try to work out what to feel or think.

'Get on, daydreamer,' laughs the girl, gesturing to the swing seat. But as she catches sight of my face, a deep crease appears between her eyebrows. 'Are you OK?'

'I don't know,' I say truthfully. 'Who are you? Where did you come from? How did you disappear, before, when I heard you calling?'

The girl smiles. 'So many questions! Come on, let's get on the swing first.'

The night is becoming stranger with each turn, and I don't know why, but I do as I'm told and sit on the swing. She leaps on behind me, slots her feet either side and stands up, pushing until we're zooming so fast through the twinkling moonlit sky that I have to grip the rope tighter. The house lights flash in and out of view as we arc through the air, cool midnight dew settling on my skin. It's like we're under a magical green bubble, better than any fairground ride, pinpricks of silver stars shining through the arching branches.

I give myself up to the flow, excitement pumping through my veins as we go faster, higher, until we're so high I think we might shoot into the night.

She lets out a throaty sound that's halfway between a yodel and a song. 'Shall we go even higher, Tamarind?'

'W-what did you say?' How can she know who I am? Suddenly I feel a little bit scared. 'How did you know my name?'

She doesn't reply. Each time the swing flies through the air the wind whips the leaves on the tree so they make a loud rustling sound . . . The garden stretches out below me, spreading into the shadowy distance and the house with its turrets sitting up on the mound, a long way away.

'What's *your* name?' I call to the girl.

It's as if the garden is holding its breath, and she pushes the swing even higher. 'Ishhhhta,' she sings.

A cloud of shimmering fireflies flutter past my head, lighting up the garden with their iridescent glow.

The swing begins to slow down and the girl – Ishta – jumps to the ground. She whistles. Hanu leaps out of the tree and grabs hold of her hand. She tickles him under the chin.

I bite my lip, trying to work things out. 'It must be nice to have a pet monkey.'

Ishta slides her arm through mine again. 'Yes . . . he's my buddy, but he's an old monkey now.' Hanu chirps as if in protest. 'Anyway, let's do something nice. Shall we go for a swim? Find some berries? We could be friends if you wanted.' Her eyes glow. 'I'd love to get to know you.'

'Mmmm . . .' I'm not sure; after all, I don't know anything about her and she doesn't seem to want to answer my questions. But clearly she knows the garden really well. She must live somewhere close by.

Without warning, tiredness comes over me like a rain cloud and I flop on to the ground, yawning, the soft sounds of frogs soothing as a lullaby. I've been out for ages tonight – and I haven't slept yet. It's got to be three or four in the morning, maybe later. 'Actually . . . I'd better get back. *And* you. You've got to get home too, haven't you?'

She doesn't reply. Instead, she gazes up at the stars and gives a long sigh.

We walk back together, skirting the edge of the wild garden, heading towards the house. As we near the hut she stops, looks towards the darkened paths that lead to the house beyond with something like longing in her eyes. Suddenly I feel bad for not playing with her more.

'Maybe you could come to the house in the morning,' I suggest. 'We can play then.'

'I can't.' She leans against the trunk of a tree, as if she's suddenly exhausted. 'But I've got something for you.' She dips a hand into her pocket and holds out a long dark pod about the length of my palm.

I hold out my hand and she drops it in there. It feels rough and slightly warm. It's really pretty. I've never seen anything like this before and examine it closely. 'Thank you. I-I don't have anything for you though, sorry.' I give the seed pod a shake and it rattles as if it has treasure hidden inside.

Her face lit up by the moon seems paler. 'It doesn't matter, but it means we're real friends now.' Her mouth curls into a smile.

'That's really kind.' I put it in my pocket. Suddenly I don't feel so alone in this strange place.

Beyond the mountains the sky is turning to light

and the stars are beginning to fade. I start to panic, remembering everything that happened tonight with the family. I have to get back before they find out that I've sneaked into the garden.

'Come back soon, won't you? At night. Meet me by the swing.' She turns back towards the archway, little Hanu, her monkey tripping along behind her, the flash of his tail disappearing into the trees.

'Wait . . . where are you going? Where do you live? Why can we only play at night?' I start to follow, but she's much too quick, and when I try to work out which way she went, I can't see her at all.

12

I sling my muddy trainers outside and slink back into the house through the unlocked verandah doors. It's still early and I'm sure there's no one about so I should get away with it.

Brushing the dirt from my hair, I tiptoe across the hallway and reach the bottom of the stairs. I'm just about to sprint up, but Uma's voice makes me freeze.

'Tamarind?' She shuffles round the corner carrying a tray piled high with starched napkins and a silver bowl full of golden globes that smell sugar-sweet. 'Look at you.' She tuts and lowers her eyes, resting them on my grubby clothes. 'You've been somewhere?'

'Um . . . no. I just wanted a drink of water.'

'Hmmph.' She narrows her eyes and comes closer. 'Chinty, too, liked to go out at night or early in the morning. You girls.'

I lean towards her. 'W-where did she used to go?'

Her eyes turn watery and she looks away for a moment and I think she's about to tell me more. 'Maybe we'll talk later, *beta* – come to the kitchen, like I said. Now . . . go and get clean before your *nanijee* sees. And here.' She picks up one of the globes of sugary dough soaked in sticky syrup and holds it under my nose.

I sniff it and eye it suspiciously. 'What is it?'

'Only *gulab jaman*. Very sweet, very yum.' She smiles. 'Try and I think you'll like.'

It smells like warm caramel. I take it from Uma and stick out my tongue to try a teeny taste. 'Mmmm . . . like doughnuts.'

'Go on,' Uma urges, smiling.

I take a little bite and lick the sticky syrup off my lips. 'Nice.' I pop the small treat into my mouth. 'You said before that Mum liked them – I can see why.' Of everyone in the family, Uma appears to be the most open to talking about Mum . . . so I ask her straight. 'Why won't anyone talk about Mum, Uma?'

I think I'm about to discover something when she lowers her voice and glances back towards the kitchen – but all she says is: 'Your *nanijee* doesn't like it. Tamarind, you need to stop asking questions.'

Disappointment comes crashing down like an

almighty wave. I'm so fed up of this. So fed up of asking about Mum and getting only silence – it's like throwing myself against a brick wall.

'Tamarind?'

I ignore Uma's gentle voice and sprint up the stairs to my bedroom as quietly as I can. I shut the door softly, afraid of waking anyone up, and pull a chair across it, suddenly desperate to be alone. I sit on the bed and try to bring the whirling events of the past two days to some sort of order, but they stay stubbornly inexplicable . . . nothing makes any sense, not the hushed voices surrounding Mum, not the girl in the garden, and not hateful Sufia who snatched the only thing I ever had of Mum's.

If I only had the ring, I don't think I'd feel so bad about everything else. I think I'd feel less lost. As soon as I put Mum's ring on I felt something shift, like memories awakening after being trapped inside that box for so long. It's as if it had been waiting for me to find it, to wear it like she did. And now . . . *Sufia* has it!

I fall into bed without bothering even to wash and, despite the rage, somehow I do sleep for a few hours. When I wake, I fling open the bathroom door and fill the tub with steaming water, stare in the mirror at my wild knotted hair, my scratched face, and vow again that I *will* get Mum's ring back.

The water is scalding but I plunge myself in, dunking right under, all the fury against Sufia pulsing back. She's probably hidden it somewhere she thinks I won't dare to go, but I want it so badly I'll do anything and go anywhere to get it.

After a few minutes, I grip the edge of the bath, haul myself out and throw on some clothes. I'm going to need some help. I hurry along the carpeted corridor to the room at the end – Arjun's room. He promised to keep my visit to the hut a secret, so maybe he'll help me get the ring back.

I tap lightly on the door and go in. Although it's quite late now, Arjun is still sleeping, one arm dangling from the covers. It's a small, cosy room, painted a warm yellow. On a shelf above his bed, he's lined up an origami zoo. I peer at the figures and make out a tiger, a swan, and maybe a dog. There are two battered skateboards hooked to the wall and a poster of a cool guy doing some sort of skate trick.

'Arjun. Wake up.' I shake him gently. 'It's me, Tamarind.'

He stirs but doesn't wake.

'Come on, sleepyhead.'

I lift the window and rattle open the shutters,

letting the morning sun into his room – at last, he opens his eyes. 'W . . . what are you doing here?' he yawns. 'It's still early, isn't it? For a holiday.'

'Arjun, I need your help.' I balance on the window ledge. 'I need to get something back from Sufia that doesn't belong to her. Will you help me?'

He's been friendly up to now but I'm not sure he'll plot against his sister with me. I hold my breath.

Arjun narrows his eyes like he's thinking. 'She's always taking things. She thinks everything belongs to her. What's she stolen this time?'

I sigh out in relief. 'It . . . it's a special ring, that belonged to my mum.' I don't tell him I found it in the hut. 'She's got it and I think she's hidden it in her room. I need to get in there and take a look. I only need you to distract her – will you?'

'Sufia's sleeping in the attic room, isn't she?' Arjun says, as we peek out of his room and into the corridor, waiting for Sufia to emerge.

I nod. 'She'll have to come down this way.'

'OK, here's the plan. Stay in your room, watching the verandah from your window,' says Arjun, sounding excited. 'Once Sufia's having breakfast I'll give you a signal and keep her there for as long as I can without it seeming weird while you search her room.

She's clever though, and she'll wonder why you aren't at breakfast . . . she'll also be expecting you to be looking for the ring, so keep alert.'

We hear a sudden creak from the top of the stairs. Sufia emerges grumpily from the attic staircase, clattering down the next set of stairs to the ground-floor hallway. Once she's gone, Arjun turns to me and gives a businesslike nod.

'Right,' says Arjun, 'back to your room. Watch for my signal!'

He shoots on down to breakfast and I hurry back to my room. I stand by the window until I spy Sufia sitting beside Nanijee, her plate piled with food. When Arjun arrives, Sufia stands up and looks around suspiciously, but he tugs at her sleeve and gets her to sit back down before giving me a quick look – the signal. I know I don't have long so I take off towards Sufia's room. Setting the timer on my watch for three minutes, I take a deep breath before opening the door, feeling like a burglar.

13

Blood thuds through my ears as I scan the room. It's tiny, more like a cupboard with a small window to one side, shelves with spare linen and neatly stacked towels. The bed is just a narrow camp bed on the floor with the battered, one-eyed teddy sitting on the pillow. Sufia must really hate me if she chose to sleep in here instead of in a proper room with me!

I ignore my feelings and start the hunt for the ring. Where would I put something if I didn't want anyone to find it? Under the bed – too easy, but I dip my head and take a look anyway. Nothing there. Her unpacked bag is still on the floor so I plunge my hands in, hoping she just slung it in last night, but it's only full of dirty clothes.

The jolly jingle of the timer makes me jump out of my skin – has it already been three minutes? I race to check under the mattress, under the pillow, between the stacked sheets, but don't find it anywhere. Frantic footsteps pound up the stairs and I shoot under the bed, heart hammering, but they fade without coming in – probably Uma visiting one of the other attic rooms. I know I should leave now but if it's in this room I might not get another chance to come back.

Or maybe she hid it somewhere else, after all.

I wriggle out, tiptoe across, have my hand on the doorknob, ready to leave, when I notice a high shelf filled with little trinkets and figures that runs all the way along the top of the wall.

With one eye on the door, my hands trembling, I drag a chair so I can stretch up to see if it's there, but I'm not tall enough. I fling Sufia's stuff from the small side table on to her bed and balance it on the chair. It wobbles as I try to stand as still as I can and look beyond the trinkets but there's nothing on that side. It feels like my stomach is full of crawling spiders but I move the chair, set it up again on the far side of the room with the table on top and clamber up as carefully as if I'm climbing Everest.

What are those little green bootees doing here, the ones that were in my room? But I'm more interested in what's tucked behind them, pushed right to the back and tied to a red ribbon: Mum's ring! I lean in as far as I dare, stretching my fingertips to reach for it, and just manage to hook it from behind the trinkets, but the chair sways beneath me and I crash on to the floor with the clay animals, vases and the bootees tumbling with me.

The door flies open. It's Sufia, followed closely by Arjun, who pushes past and kneels beside me.

'Get out of my room,' bellows Sufia, nostrils flaring, anger puffing out of her like icy breath. She stoops to the ground and delicately picks up the bootees. 'I said, *get out*!' Her livid face turns blazing red.

'Leave her alone,' says Arjun, standing between us. 'You've been really horrible to Tamarind.'

For a moment Sufia's face changes, as if she's genuinely upset, just like it did in the hut. Her lip trembles, but then as if she's putting on a mask, the temper returns and she gives Arjun the evil eye.

She strides over and tries to grab the ring again. 'Give it to me . . . this doesn't belong to you.'

I'm shaking, pain and anger coursing through my body. I can't keep the tears back any longer and they track down my cheeks like hot lava. 'No . . . I won't give it to you.' I slip the ring on my finger. 'You snatched it from me before but this time I'm keeping it . . . I know you don't care,' I sob, 'but it's my mum's. It's the only thing I have of hers and I can't give it up.'

'And you know you haven't got anyone to turn to,' says Arjun, folding his arms and standing firm. 'Nanijee will be really upset with you and so will Mum and Dad . . . and you know you're on your final warning after your school reports.'

'Why are you taking her side?' Despite her shaved and dyed hair, Sufia suddenly looks really young. Her lip begins to tremble properly this time.

'She's our guest, Sufia,' says Arjun, moving closer to me. '*And* she's nice to me.'

Sufia stands tall, her hands on her hips as she turns to me. 'So you want to know about your mum, do you?' she whispers, her eyes glistening. She's looking really odd and I think again that maybe she's going to cry, but then she puts her mean face back on. 'Well, I'll tell you the thing that no one else wants to tell you.' She says each word with a slow menace that makes my palms slippery with sweat.

'Sufia, please,' says Arjun, trying to squeeze between us, to shield me from Sufia's glare.

My heart feels like a hammer punching at my ribs, my mouth as dry as dust.

Sufia laughs and shoves Arjun out of the way so

she's back in my face. 'I knew your mum for ages before you came along. She played with me, sang me songs, painted elephants on my nursery wall and rocked me to sleep. She died when I was six, but I remember her really clearly.'

Tears prick against my eyelids but I won't let them out. I clench my jaw tight and look away from her. I wanted to know about Mum – but not like this. Arjun has given up trying to stop her and stands against a bookshelf, chewing the side of his mouth and looking at the floor like he'd rather be anywhere else.

'Everything was fantastic until she met your dad. Do you know how angry the whole family was when you came along?' She spits her words out and they scorch me with their fire.

'Sufia—' Arjun begins to speak.

'Shut up!' she yells. 'Just shut up!' I don't think Sufia can come any closer but now she's pressed right against me, her nose practically touching mine. She looks down at me and thunders at the top of her voice. 'She died because of you!'

I collapse against the wall, my insides caving in, my head spinning. 'What? Why didn't anyone say . . . ?'

Sufia's eyes glint with triumph. 'Of course no one

ever told you . . . They're protecting you, stupid. Because it's all your fault! She died in childbirth, Tamarind. She died so you could live. You. Killed. Her.'

I put my hands over my ears. 'Stop, stop. You're lying. It's not true.' I lift my tear-stained face. 'Arjun?' I whisper. 'It's not true, is it?'

Arjun doesn't answer.

'Get out!' bellows Sufia, her face a beacon of fire. 'It's not over between us, nosy, interfering English girl,' she hisses.

She pushes Arjun and I on to the landing and slams her door shut.

14

I'm back in my room, sitting against the hard wall beside the bed, alone after telling Arjun to give me some time on my own for a bit. Downstairs I can hear Uma singing as she bustles around in the kitchen, the smell of sizzling onions seeping through the floorboards. Aunt Simran and Nani are sitting out on the verandah, chatting and reading the newspaper Auntie bought from the village yesterday. Even up here I can hear the beat of Kamaal's music thudding through the house.

But although it's been an hour or more since Sufia spat out the truth at me, her words are still ringing in my ears and I can't make them go away. Salt-dried tears crust my blotchy face like scars. I'm glad: I want everyone to see them. The big secret that no one ever told me is that *I* am the reason Mum died.

The reality smashes through me and I clench my

fists so hard my knuckles turn white.

I touch the green stone of the ring and imagine Mum wearing it, looking at it just as I am. I'm desperate to wear it all the time, to feel close to her, but I don't want Nani to see it and get upset, so I put it in my pocket and zip it up safely.

'Hey,' says Arjun, stepping in softly. 'You'd better come down, or everyone will start getting worried.' He shifts his feet awkwardly. 'I've never seen Sufia so mean,' he mutters. 'And I didn't know . . . you know . . . that thing about you and . . . and your mum.'

'D-do you know what happened after? A . . . after Mum died? Why do they all hate Dad?'

'I don't know really . . . I mean, nobody tells *me* anything and I wasn't even born then. But they sometimes say things when they think I'm not listening.'

'Like what?'

Arjun looks away at the window. 'Like how Nani-jee wanted to keep you here, but your dad took you away. It made everyone really sad, I think, the whole thing. He broke the family up, that's what they say.'

'But why is Sufia especially mad with me?'

'She was really close to your mum when she was little. She went everywhere with her. Apparently, when it happened she stopped eating and wouldn't stop crying and asking where she'd gone.' He flops against the pillows. 'That's just what Sufia told me and what I've overheard – I don't know much really.'

'I'm sorry to keep asking questions.' I can tell he's had enough and I can't blame him – he's only young and I'm sure he's dying to get away.

'I'm starving, is it lunchtime yet?' he asks, fidgeting with the edge of the duvet.

My stomach gives a growl, reminding me that I haven't eaten in ages. 'You go ahead. I'll be down in a minute.'

Arjun leaps off the bed. 'See you there,' he says, bolting through the door.

Even though I'm hungry, the last thing I feel like doing is sitting at the table surrounded by everyone again, but I know they'll start asking questions if I'm not there. I've already missed breakfast.

In the bathroom, I quickly run cold water and splash my face, trying to cool my sore cheeks. Bloodshot eyes stare back at me in the mirror as I try to smooth down my tangled mess of hair.

I have to find out more about what happened and why nobody apart from Sufia will talk about it. Sunday will be here soon and Dad will be back to take me home. This week is my only chance to uncover all the secrets and finally get to the truth. I take a deep breath.

'I've been looking for you,' says Aunt Simran, who is walking up the stairs as I open my bedroom door. 'I was worried – you were really quiet yesterday and then you didn't come down for breakfast.' She strokes my hair, notices my eyes. 'Are you all right?'

I wish I could, but I can't tell her the truth – I'll get in trouble. 'I-I've been really tired,' I stammer. 'And I wasn't hungry this morning, I just wanted to sleep.'

She puts an arm around my shoulder. 'We all love you, Tamarind. We've missed you. I know the food here is hard for you, so Uma's made some plain scrambled eggs with hot buttery toast for your lunch. Does that sound good?'

I give her a small smile. 'Thank you – I'm sure I'll get used to things but I'm just a bit of a fusspot, as Dad says.' After the news from Sufia, I don't think I could eat anything.

'Come on.'

We walk slowly down the stairs together, Aunt Simran still holding me close. Part of me wants to run away again, not sure if Aunt Simran is just better at hiding her true feelings than Sufia, but she seems so kind. I keep thinking how me being here must be so hard for everyone.

I think back to the girl in the garden; maybe Aunt Simran might know her. 'There was a girl,' I begin – then pause. I can't tell her I went out in the night. 'In the garden, you know, when I . . . when I got upset on Monday night and ran off.'

'You must have seen Sufia – she goes out there often.' She sighs. 'I'm glad it's only her you saw. Tamarind, don't go into the garden again after dark. This isn't England. We have wild animals out here in the mountains, dangerous animals.'

I ignore the warning and continue. 'It wasn't Sufia. This girl was around my age – she said her name is Ishta. I thought maybe she lived nearby?'

Aunt Simran frowns as we reach the bottom of the stairs. 'Nobody lives around here apart from us, Tamarind. The closest village takes ages to get to without a car. Look how tired you are – could you have dreamt it?'

I know I didn't dream it – but sometimes you can tell you're going to get in trouble if you don't agree with a grown-up. So I nod: 'I guess so.'

We reach the dining room, but Aunt Simran hesitates outside. 'You know, Ishta is the name for a person's favourite deity, or goddess.' She smiles. 'Do you like myths and legends? Have a look in your room – you might find a book or two that interests you.'

We go on to the verandah, Aunt Simran guiding me away from the grand velvet chair. 'Come and sit by Nani.'

Arjun is wolfing down a piece of toast, his plate half empty already. Kamaal's headphones are blasting a drumbeat as he eats.

'Kamaal,' scolds Nani, waving at him to get his attention. 'No headphones at the table. How many times do I say it?'

He pushes them off his head. 'OK, Nanijee,' he laughs and carries on eating.

'And where's Sufia?' Nani says. 'I hope she's not still sulking. She ran off upstairs really fast after breakfast.'

'I'll go up and see her,' says Aunt Simran. 'Give her some TLC. Carry on with lunch, everyone.'

Arjun frowns and concentrates on his food.

'Tamarind, *beta*,' continues Nani. 'You look so tired. Some fresh air after lunch and then a nap.'

I press my fingers against the cold cutlery, try to swallow the sadness about how Mum died and force a smile. 'OK, Nani.'

Uma comes in carrying the plate of scrambled egg and toast and puts it in front of me. 'I made these extra special, so you must eat. There's nothing spicy, nothing strange, only egg and butter.'

Even though the bombshell Sufia hurled at me earlier means tears are only a blink away, I'm feeling shaky and know I have to eat. I plunge the fork into the creamy pile of egg and force it into my mouth.

Uma rubs my back. 'I knew you would eat them, and for dinner I have something else for you to try.'

I remember the sweet treat she gave me earlier. I feel bad at how I left things with her, running away when she told me not to talk about Mum. I try hard to smile and tell her 'thank you'. Whatever she's got in mind for dinner might just be OK.

After lunch is finished, Nani begins watering the pots on the verandah, Aunt Simran and Uma pore over a shopping list, deciding what to cook later, and Kamaal heads out to meet up with friends. Me and Arjun kick a football around on the grass again, but I can't concentrate properly and make an excuse to go up to my room. I want to check out the books I saw above my bed on the first night. Aunt Simran suggested there may be something there on Ishta.

When I get upstairs, I glance through the titles on the shelf over my bed – sure enough, there's a book on ancient gods and goddesses. I pull it off and blow away a layer of dust as I settle on the bed.

I slip Mum's ring from my zipped pocket and put

it on. It catches the sunlight, sending sparkling beams across the walls of the room. It's as if Mum's right here with me. I take the photo from the bedside table and hold it in my palm. The rays from the ring reflect a rainbow light on to the photo.

I snuggle into bed and turn the first yellowing page.

15

Mum's name is written in careful curved writing across the inside cover of the book.

Chinty

It's bordered by rows of stars. This was Mum's book! I hold it tight before reading, a buzz of excitement leaping in my chest. Then I open the index and see if I can find an entry for Ishta . . . I find one for *Ishtar* instead, so flick to the page.

The Myth of Ishtar

Ishtar is an ancient goddess who was first written about in the texts of Mesopotamia – she is the first deity for whom researchers have discovered written evidence. She is powerful and is usually seen in the company of owls to show her wisdom, and lions to show her strength . . .

I recall the statue at the entrance to the wild garden – it sounds like it's the same goddess, the goddess Ishtar. I carry on reading.

> Ishtar lends her name to the morning star. In the West she is known as Venus, but Ishtar came first. All the stories of Venus, the evening and morning star, originate with the myths of the Middle East . . .

I flick further on, to the beautiful paintings of the goddess, examining them closely. They're all different, showing her having adventures in the mountains, by a lake, in a deep forest, surrounded by flocks of animals and birds.

But what about Ishta? I think. *Didn't Aunt Simran say it was a name for a favourite deity?*

I yawn, wanting to read more about the goddess, but I can't keep my eyes open any longer and they droop closed, sending me off into a deep sleep, empty of dreams.

I'm woken by a knock on the door. 'Are you OK? You've slept *all afternoon*!' says Arjun, walking into the room. 'I came up earlier but you were still asleep. I wanted to cheer you up after what Sufia said to you.' He sits on the spare bed. 'I made you another friend.' He puts one of his origami figures on the bedside table.

'Is it a lion?' I yawn, sitting up.

'Yes!' He sounds really pleased. 'Last time I made one, Sufia said it looked like a rat.'

I remember the line from the book about how Ishtar was always shown with lions, to symbolize her strength. Maybe this is a sign that I have to be strong too. 'Thank you, that's really sweet. And I'm fine. At least I know a bit more about what happened. It's better to know things sometimes, even though they might upset you. At least you can start dealing with it – Dad kept it all from me.'

'Do you want me to show you round the house before dinner? You haven't been given a tour yet.'

Even though I feel like I could sleep for longer, I agree. Arjun must've been bored all afternoon by himself. 'That'll be fun, thanks.' I take Mum's ring off and hide it safely in my pocket again.

Chacha Dev is fixing the latch on a bedroom door as we dive past him and zoom further up the stairs, the sound of Nani and Aunt Simran's chatter rising from the dining room.

Arjun leads me through the old, creaky house, starting at the top, right by the cupboard room that Sufia's sleeping in. The door is closed and there's some music blaring from behind it. We tiptoe past, then run to the other end of the corridor where there's another flight of stairs that go up into a narrow circular tower and also lead downstairs. We head up. The room at the top is really cool with a great view over the orchard, the chickens and the cow that's munching at the grass.

'This is one of the towers,' says Arjun, his face lighting up with a grin. 'Sometimes when I have friends to stay we pretend we're trapped in a castle and make up stories about lions, heroes and hidden treasure.' He walks over to a big old chest and lifts the lid. 'Look, this is our dressing-up box.' The clothes inside are colourful and jumbled.

'That's so cool,' I say.

'Maybe we can play later?' he asks hopefully.

I smile. 'Maybe.' But my mind drifts to my adventures in the garden with Ishta.

Once we've been all over the house we end up back by my room. From the window on the landing, the first star of the evening shines fiercely beside the moon and I think of Ishtar, the goddess from the book. Tonight, I'll go find the girl in the garden.

At dinner we have the usual routine of everyone in their places, Kamaal with his headphones on – headphones off, when Nani shoots him a dark look –

Sufia giving me the eye and Aunt Simran keeping her in check, and of course the lonely wooden chair with the turquoise velvet back, waiting for its owner.

The table is overloaded with food, steaming dishes dotted along the middle again, and I'm beginning to get used to the fragrant smells, the spiced tea and the saffron-scented rice.

Uma brings a small dish covered with a lid and puts it proudly in front of me. 'This is the special dish I was talking about.'

Sufia looks the other way and crinkles her nose.

I ignore Sufia and lift the lid. It's yellow rice with fat raisins scattered over, chunks of chopped coconut and slices of orange mango. My stomach lunges. It's the opposite of plain. 'Thank you, Uma.'

'It's sweet,' says Uma. 'You are a sweet one. Try it.'

I take a spoonful and slowly take a bite. To my surprise, I like it. She's right: it is sweet. 'Yum,' I say, surprised to find myself preparing another mouthful.

'You taste the cardamom? The *leaychi*?'

'Yes . . . it's crunchy . . . it's nice.' I glance up at Uma, who's beaming. 'I really like it!'

After dinner, I tell everyone I need to catch up on more sleep, so go up to my room early. Instead, as soon as it's dark I creep into the garden again. Aunt

Simran thinks I was imagining that girl but I'm going to prove to myself that she's real.

I take out the long seed pod she gave me as a present. It feels solid as I hold it between my fingers and give it a shake, the tiny treasures inside making a rattling sound as the seeds hit the shell. And I know I didn't imagine her: she's a real solid girl, just like the gift she gave me, and I feel a warm buzz spread through me.

The midnight sky is ablaze with scattered stars, the curve of the moon bold and bright. I take Mum's ring from my pocket and put it on my finger – I hold it ahead of me and it seems to glow as if it's lit from the inside, the vivid green stone stirring me awake.

I hear the song again, faint and echoing, mingling with the breeze – *Taaaamarind* . . .

I hurry through the garden filled with new energy, stamp across the nettles, past the rock and finally through the copse until I'm right by the hut, where dear little Hanu, Ishta's golden monkey, seems to be waiting for me. He takes my hand and leads me under the stone arch with the goddess perched on top, tripping further until we're deep in the tangled wild garden, where we follow the path round just as before.

My heart gives a little leap, because she's there as clear as anything, standing under the tree. Hanu leaves me and, giving a squeal of joy, rushes to Ishta's side.

'I came back,' I say, trying to catch my breath, 'just like you wanted and I brought you a present.' I've been thinking about something I can give her in return for the pretty seed pod. I unpin my Arsenal badge from my sweatshirt and hold it out to her.

'What is it?'

'It's my special football badge. I got it when I made the First Team.'

She takes it and smiles, looks at it closely. Ishta pins the badge to her waistcoat. There's a moment of stillness and then she glances up to meet my eyes. 'Thank you.'

'When I first got here,' I begin, 'I was playing football with my cousin Arjun and I chased the ball almost to the wild garden.'

She looks at me thoughtfully. 'Yes?'

'Well, I heard something – like a song. It was strange. I was wondering, w-was it you? Singing, I mean?'

She crinkles her nose thoughtfully. 'The breezes in the Himalaya carry for miles, perhaps it was the song of some bird.'

I nod – but I'm not convinced. I think of the song now . . . it definitely sounded like a human voice to me.

16

After a pause, Ishta asks, 'So . . . you like football?'
'Yeah! I love it. I play it all the time back home.' I grin and pretend I have a ball, dribble around her, tapping her foot. 'This is how you tackle, now try and get the ball from me.'

She laughs and plays along, running a little circle around me. 'Like this?' She jostles forward, knocking the imaginary ball from me, and running ahead a few paces before stopping. 'You must be fit,' she pants. 'I'm all puffed out!'

'You weren't bad,' I say, laughing. 'I think the Arsenal badge helped.'

Ishta steps towards me and puts a hand on my arm. 'You've got kind eyes,' she continues, 'hasn't she, Hanu? And lovely long hair. My ma likes me to tie mine up, but maybe I could wear it all out and flowing like yours one day.'

She's wearing the flowery embroidered dress again with the loose trousers underneath, a sheepskin waistcoat over the top and her dagger in a sheath slung around her hips.

'I like your outfit . . . it's fun,' I say.

She touches the Arsenal badge, like she's really proud to be wearing something I gave her. It looks a bit weird against her outlandish clothing and I giggle.

She laughs too. 'Let's explore the garden, do something exciting like real friends?'

Even though I hardly know this girl I want to be her friend so badly. I feel the same as I did the first time I met Rafi; I knew we were going to be friends for ever through everything. Fire blazes through me, like an electric buzz going all over, right to the tips of my fingers.

'Come on, take hold of Hanu's hand,' Ishta says.

I do as she asks, feel the monkey's little hand clutch mine. 'Let's go,' I shout, kicking at a giant pine cone as if it were a football. 'Passing!' I yell, dribbling it towards Ishta. She traps it with her toe, giggles, and kicks it back. 'Not bad,' I say, pushing Aunt Simran's warnings, of wolves, tigers and other wild animals away again.

We continue through the garden, passing the pine cone between us.

Hanu joins in and grabs it.

'Hey – handball.'

He chatters and rolls the pine cone ahead and we rush forward, ducking under low branches, jumping over pyramids of leaves, kicking the pine cone into new corners I didn't know were here last time, until we're out of breath and have to stop.

'You're getting pretty good at football,' I say.

'Maybe if I practised I could get as good as you,' says Ishta, watching as I show off some of the tricks I learnt at camp.

I kick the pine cone and it goes off into the distance, landing between two thick tree trunks. 'Goal!' I jump up and down and Ishta does a victory dance.

She holds her side, her breath puffing out of her. 'That was fun.'

We've ended up beside a dilapidated old green-house, and when I shine the torch towards it the light bounces off its shattered windows.

'Shall we climb it?' Ishta says. 'Be careful though, I don't want you to cut yourself.'

Weeds have threaded themselves, serpent-like, around the broken door and run riot all over its sloped roof, in and out of the cracked glass.

Hanu leaps on to the greenhouse and Ishta follows

him, nimble as a mountain goat, hooking her foot into a glass-less window frame to push herself up on to the fragile roof.

I hesitate for a second, watching shadows shifting with the moon. Even though I've climbed trees since I was little, this seems a bit more dangerous.

'Come on, you can do it.'

I shake off my worries and feel the wind whipping through my hair.

'I'm coming,' I laugh, hoicking myself up, avoiding the jagged panes of glass. Hanu claps his hands, jumps down to the ground and watches as I climb higher until I'm sitting beside Ishta. The monkey hurries back up, sits between us and strokes my cheek.

'Do you want to see something special?' asks Ishta, excitement blooming across her face.

'OK,' I reply, following her as we climb carefully down from the roof of the greenhouse and leap back into the garden.

Holding Hanu's hands between us again, we sprint to the very furthest end of the garden, where a high hedge runs all the way round, protecting it from the mountain wilderness beyond.

Ishta drops Hanu's hand and begins searching for something in the hedge, scanning low down between the fine twisty stems. 'Lend me your torch. It's down here somewhere.'

'What is?'

'Just wait and see,' she giggles. 'There!' She shines the torch on a gap in the hedge and drops to her knees, shuffling towards it. 'We can get out this way and explore the mountains. I know a shepherd's hut we can shelter in if we need to. Come here.'

I crouch beside her and peer through the hedge at the mountains, the rugged landscape that has a different scent, a cooler breeze.

'Look,' she says, pointing the torch into the distance.

Swirls of grey mist hangs above a wide dark lake where a small rowing boat tied to a tree branch not too far from us shifts in the breeze, the water flapping against its hull.

'Come on. Not scared, are you?'

Only now do Aunt Simran's warnings bang at my brain and I suddenly come to my senses.

'No. O-of course I'm not scared. I just . . . I'm not sure this is a good idea, that's all.'

'It's OK, you know, you're allowed to be scared. After all, it's your first time this far. We don't have to go through, not this time anyway.' She puts an arm around my shoulder. 'But look, over there.'

'I don't see anything.'

I follow Ishta's finger through the hedge, to the far side of the lake, lit up by the moon.

'You have to squeeze your eyes together and *really* look.'

I do as she says and concentrate hard and then I see a shifting of shapes like a dark moving clump, a silhouette of hunched animals, like dogs but bigger. One throws back its head and lets out a deep howl.

'Wolves. They've got cubs,' says Ishta excitedly. 'When you're more used to it here, we can go and see them . . . Don't worry.' She brings her face close to mine. 'I won't let anything happen to you. I've got my dagger just in case.'

Hanu begins to whimper and wraps his arms around Ishta's waist. 'Don't be silly, they're only wolves – wild animals just like you.'

My heart speeds up. 'M . . . maybe next time.'

Ishta nods, then says, 'I know! Let's go on the swing again.'

We leave the gap in the hedge and go back to the safety of the garden, back the way we came until we're beside the tree, the house lights in the distance welcoming us home.

We rush under the canopy of dark leaves and Ishta climbs on to the swing, like she did before. I sit, grasping the rope between my fingers and we begin flying through the air, the soft wind blowing against my face.

'I wish I could leave,' she cries, making the swing go higher and higher. 'I'd love to explore the world, see what's out there. It would be so exciting.'

'Why don't you?'

'I can't.' She lets the swing slow down until it comes to a stop and she jumps off. She lifts Hanu on to her hip. He's quite big and she struggles to hold him. 'We can't leave, can we, Hanu? This is our home.' She puts the monkey back on the ground. 'For ever.'

'But no one else lives around here,' I say, stepping closer. 'Only my family. My aunt said so. Where did you come from?'

She stares at the moon, at the bright star that sits next to it.

'I'm not lying,' she says, as though the words are snagging her throat.

'I think that's Venus,' I say, joining her, looking up at the sky. *The morning star, Ishtar*, I think, remembering the line in the book. I'm about to tell her what Aunt Simran told me about her name but she interrupts.

'I like your ring. Can I see?'

I'm not sure that I really want to part with it, especially after what happened with Sufia, but I really like Ishta and I'm sure she'll give it back.

I take it off my finger and hand it to her. It's glowing in the clear night sky, the beams of light illuminating her pretty face, her high cheekbones and straight nose. She looks familiar somehow, in a way I haven't noticed before.

'Can I try it on?'

I nod.

She puts it on the exact same finger as I wore it on. 'Perfect fit,' she smiles.

'It belonged to my mum.'

She peers at the ring. For a moment, I think she looks older than she is – her expression is really serious and grown-up. 'It's beautiful. An emerald, I think. The Himalaya are famous for emeralds and some people say there are a few special stones that carry a magical power. Maybe this is one of those.'

I open my eyes wider. 'It does seem to glow . . .' I say softly. 'Almost like it's pointing somewhere.'

Ishta nods. 'And look at the work that's gone into making the stone sparkle. A very special person would have made this for your ma.'

She holds the ring towards the starlight, its eight-pointed silver star mirroring the one shining in the sky. Ishta brushes her arm close to mine and I feel her warmth. She has blood pumping through her veins just like me and I know she's real, not a part of my imagination as Aunt Simran seemed to think. I give her a huge smile and move even closer.

The emerald stone lights up her face and she gives me a smile. 'Look how the ring shines, Tamarind. This was made with such love.'

17

Me and Ishta step outside the canopy of the tree into the wild garden. She takes off the ring and hands it back.

Ishta looks up at the sky again, at the clouds scudding across the stars. And suddenly she frowns.

'What's wrong?' I ask her. 'I thought you were happy.'

'There's a storm coming,' she says, narrowing her eyes and holding tight to Hanu's hand. 'We won't be able to play once it's here. I *am* happy though,' she continues. She steps close, looking into my eyes as if she's searching for something. 'Tamarind, some nights I might not be here . . . and sometime, I don't know when, I might have to go away . . . for ever. But I need you to know that no matter what, I'll always be your friend. Do you understand?'

I feel a patter of rain splash my face. I don't

understand at all, but I nod slightly, realizing she's waiting for me to agree.

Ishta steps backwards, Hanu taking her hand.

'I had a really nice time tonight,' I say. 'Thank you.'

But her face has lost its glow and she looks pale and tired. Hanu gives one of his high-pitched screams and tugs at her hand.

'So did I,' she murmurs. 'Come back, won't you? When the sky is clear.'

When I look again, she's disappeared. I run a few hurried steps in her direction, but the only thing I see is a flash of gold, like jewelled dust motes suspended in the night.

The house is in darkness when I get in, except for a warm candle glow coming from the kitchen. I'm even more confused than ever about Ishta. Why was she saying she couldn't leave even though she wanted to go exploring? And if she can't leave, why those ominous words about never coming back? I'm about to take the stairs up to my bedroom, but the light from the kitchen is drawing me in. Uma has been with the family for ever and she keeps telling me to come and see her – maybe she'll tell me more about my mum. I might know the horrible truth about how she died, thanks to Sufia, but I still don't feel like I *know* her at all. I twist Mum's ring – it's dull in the clouded night – and take a few quiet steps towards the open door.

'Come on in, Tamarind,' says Uma, without turning round. She carries on stirring the steaming pot on the cooker.

I kick at the floor with my trainer, the knots in my stomach tightening.

'Tamarind,' she says, still concentrating on stirring. 'Why are you up so late?' Finally she turns to face me, glancing at the floor. 'And where have you been?'

I ignore her questions but step closer, sniffing the cloud of fragrant steam rising from the pot. 'I . . . I know you're not meant to talk about it, but I need to know about Mum . . . Dad will be back on Sunday and nobody will tell me anything.' I want to say, *except Sufia*, but I don't want to think about what she said.

Uma looks doubtful.

'I won't tell anyone, I promise . . . it's important.'

She holds my hands between her smooth palms. 'Oh, Tamarind . . . it's such a sad story. When I was a girl, I used to live in the mountains around here . . .' She brings me towards her and snuggles me in her shawl. 'When Chinty was small and woke with bad dreams, this was the only thing that would soothe her.'

The shawl is soft and the sweet scents in the kitchen comforting; for a moment I feel safe, but then I remember about how Mum died and think that even Uma must hate me for taking her away.

'What was she like?'

She tightens the shawl and cups my face in her hands. Uma is lost in her thoughts, her wrinkled forehead set in a deep frown.

'When she was young she was so sweet and loving,' she begins. 'She would always collect fruit and flowers from the garden and bring them to me. And as she got older she became quite independent.' Uma looks at the dark door even though it's closed, as if expecting someone to walk in.

I take a deep breath of air and feel a tickle twitch up my spine.

'She was a bit like Sufia.'

My chest tightens and I'm disappointed that Uma didn't say she was like me.

'Go on,' I say, my throat grazed.

She lowers her voice. 'And then the arguments started. The teenage years brought lots of fire and later – and not just when she met Raju, your papa, while he was on holiday here from England – she wanted to leave home. Even before,' Uma pauses, 'before she had you. She made your papa promise that they'd go away and live together in England, but instead of taking her, she died, and he took you.'

I bow my head, feeling sad and tired.

'But let me tell you about the happier times,' Uma continues, hugging me close. 'Chinty loved playing in the garden and she loved to go exploring . . . she even used to go out at night. She was out all hours, a real adventurer.' Uma laughs. 'She even persuaded your *babajee* to teach her to shoot arrows. And she was really impressive – with her papa's teaching she could shoot even further and higher than him.' She wipes her eyes. 'He loved her so much. We *all* loved her, tantrums and everything.' Uma stares down at my hand and touches the ring. 'You found it then? Chinty's ring.'

I feel my face flush.

'It fits perfectly.' She smiles. 'It suits you, just like it suited her.'

'Where did the ring come from?' Ishta's comments earlier intrigued me and I'm sure Uma can tell me more.

'Now there's a happy story.' She smiles. 'Chinty's papa – your *babajee* – found the stone. He was an archaeologist and he used to take her into the mountains on his explorations. One day they found a special emerald. It was made into this ring in Jaipur by an expert jeweller. And because she loved the goddess Ishtar she asked for it to have this silver star around it. Like the star of Ishtar – you know? The evening star.'

I blink. Why does it feel like that name is everywhere at the moment? 'Is Ishtar or Ishta a common name around here?'

'Not really . . . Why?'

'Oh, nothing. It was just a book I read. It seemed like an unusual name,' I say quickly. I don't want another grown-up to suspect I'm making things up. 'I love the ring so much,' I say, touching the star on my finger. 'But I know I mustn't let Nani see it. I've been keeping it safe in my pocket during the daytime.'

Uma smiles. 'We thought it had been lost. No one could find it. Until *you* came. Since *you* arrived there's something different about the house, the gardens, like it's waking up again. I can feel . . .'

'Feel what?'

'N-nothing,' says Uma. 'I'm sorry . . . I've already said too much.' Her mouth is pinched shut and I know I won't find out any more about Mum now.

18

'Come on, help me collect the pickles. Chinty used to like that. And if you're not too tired we could make something I think you'll like.'

There's a door to one side of the kitchen with a couple of rickety steps down into a cellar filled with the shadowy shapes of boxes stacked up in neat piles. Old books dotted with bird-droppings are pushed against the walls and an ancient rocking horse with a scary-looking carved head stands in the middle of the room.

Uma presses the switch, lighting up the room, which smells of deep earth and the sharp scent of vinegar. Jars of ruby-red jellies and jams line a row of pristine shelves.

'I have to start cooking, making food for Sunday.' She smiles. 'I like to cook late at night, when it's quiet and cool.'

My heart taps against my chest. Sunday. My birthday and the day Dad and Chloe come to collect me. How is it already so soon? It's Thursday tomorrow and I haven't found out half as much about Mum as I wanted to.

'This one.' She lifts a large jar filled with a rich brown chutney. 'Can you hold it?'

I take the jar in both hands, my ring flashing against the glass.

Uma lifts a squat jar with yellow pear-shaped fruits submerged in an amber liquid. 'Quince.' She's beaming now. 'For the birthday party . . . *your* birthday.'

'There's going to be a party?' I say, feeling warm and tingly.

'Of course!'

We take the jars back into the kitchen and Uma rolls up her sleeves. 'Would you like to make your own *samosa*? You can choose whatever you want to fill it with.' She plonks a silver basin brimming with freshly kneaded dough on to the big kitchen table. 'Sit.' She pulls up a stool. 'Take a little piece of dough like this.' She pinches the size of a golf ball and claps it about in her palm until it's a tight little mound and hands it to me. 'Now with the rolling pin make it thin and round – don't worry, maybe yours will be not so round.'

I set about rolling out the dough until it's sort of circular and grows to the size of a large jam-jar lid.

Uma puts it into the crook of my hand and folds it into a cone shape. 'Now you can choose.' She points to the bowls lined up on the table. 'Potato, peas, onion and any of these spices.'

I choose potato and peas and scoop them into the dough.

'Any spice? Maybe just a little?'

'No . . . I don't think so.'

'Not the cardamom you liked in the rice?'

'Er . . . maybe, that was nice.'

Uma takes a tiny pinch from a tray and sprinkles it on to the filling. 'And now with a little water close the top of the dough.'

She shuffles over to the stove where a pot of yellow oil is simmering. 'Bring your *samosa* over.'

I carry it proudly and give it to Uma, who drops it into the hot oil which crackles and bubbles, turning the pale pastry crisp and golden in a few minutes.

She fishes it out and pops it on to a plate with a square of white kitchen paper, and once the oil has been soaked up she puts it on a clean plate with a dollop of the dark chutney we brought up from the cellar.

I pull a face and Uma laughs. 'I've got a feeling

that you might like this chutney. Don't take too much — it's just a sauce, just a little dip. It's sour though, so try a small bit first — only if you want.'

'What is it?' I ask, wrinkling my nose.

'It's called *imilie*.'

As I break open the *samosa*, steam puffs out and the cardamom-scented potato and peas smell strangely appetizing. After all the running about in the garden, I'm feeling weak with hunger. I dunk it into the *imilie* chutney and stuff it into my mouth.

'Yum.' I actually like it, and even the chutney is strangely delicious.

I grab a spoon and eat it straight from the plate.

Uma's eyebrows make two high arches. 'Well well. You're not as fussy as you think!'

'I know it's sour,' I laugh, 'and I've no idea why, but I love it!'

Uma gives a mysterious smile. 'I think it's time for your bed. And remember, make sure you keep the ring hidden.'

19

I'm woken by the flapping shutters and fierce draught billowing under the bedroom door. There's a din of noise, the scraping of furniture outside on the verandah and raised voices calling out instructions as if something is going on.

Hazy light cracks into the room, spooling on to the bedclothes, and I bundle the duvet round me. The lights on my watch read two in the afternoon and I panic when I realize I've missed half the day! The family will start thinking I'm trying to avoid them.

I spring up and scan the room, in case there's some other new thing left for me to find, like the petals that appeared on my bed, but I don't see anything, just feel that sensation again, as if I'm being watched.

I hurry from the warm bed and head to the bathroom, quickly scrub the garden dirt off and glance at the face in the mirror that looks like it belongs to a different girl. I briefly touch the worry frowns between my eyebrows that seem to be getting deeper, notice the dark lines under my eyes.

It's strange what Uma was saying last night about everything being different since I arrived, but why did she stop and what did she mean?

Something flits in the mirror, a swift movement behind me, and that tickle again travelling up my spine.

Tamarind . . .

I shake off the dream that's still twirling around my head and pull on leggings and a big jumper, and get ready to face the table downstairs. I remember what Sufia whispered to me outside her room yesterday morning, how it wasn't over between us, and my heart begins to thump.

On the red rug, there's more glittery dust, imprints of small feet scampering across it. I press my hands against the shapes and when I look again there's nothing, only the rug, as clean and dust-free as ever. Did I imagine it?

My insides have turned jittery and when I get downstairs everyone is rushing about, bringing chairs in off the lawn.

Arjun runs up to me, beaming. 'You're up at last! I've been waiting to show you how to make the origami animals.'

'Sorry, Arjun,' I say, smiling a thank-you as Uma pops the ever-present plate of toast in front of me.

'There's going to be a storm,' he adds excitedly, 'so we're eating inside later.' And then in a low whisper, he says, 'I told Mum what Sufia said and Nanijee knows as well. They're not happy with her at all.'

Sufia darts me a shrivelling look as she carries in one of the chairs.

The wind is madly shaking at the trees, and way above the mountains dark clouds are hovering, joining together to make bigger storm clouds.

It's dinner time, and I feel useless as I stand in the darkened dining room and watch Uma's husband, Dev, wind down the shutters on the verandah, while leaves blow in from the garden and scatter on the floor. 'Make sure the windows and shutters are closed in your room.' He winks at me. 'Monsoon storms are the worst, but so long as we batten down the hatches all will be good.'

Aunt Simran walks over and I murmur an apology for sleeping so long, causing extra work for Uma, and not having helped bring in the chairs.

'Don't be silly! I'm pleased you're catching up on sleep. It's normal, just your body still getting used to a different time zone. Nothing to worry about,' says Aunt Simran. 'Now, Tamarind, will you light the candles please? And Arjun can you help too? Best not to put the lights on, just in case everything blows.'

'Here,' calls Arjun, throwing me a box of matches from the ornate wooden sideboard. 'We can start at the ends and meet in the middle.'

The table is long and covered in a red tablecloth, two tall vases with flowers from the garden at either end. We light the candles that are dotted along the length and it feels like Christmas, with the scent of cinnamon wafting through the open doors.

Uma brings a big plate loaded with more toast plus scrambled eggs and puts it down alongside a smaller plate with a *samosa* and the sour chutney I tried in the kitchen last night. 'Here's your special dinner, Tamarind. The *samosa* is your recipe.'

The eggs look amazing, nearly as much as Dad makes for both of us at the weekend, and I'm looking forward to the *samosa*, feeling proud of myself for trying and liking something new.

Nani steps inside and shoos everyone to their places. 'Thank you, Dev,' she says, surveying the closed and shuttered windows. 'What would we do without you?'

'My pleasure,' he smiles, bringing in the velvet

chair from the verandah – the chair that no one ever sits on – and tucking it in at the end before leaving the room.

'Come on, let's eat,' says Aunt Simran as Uma brings in more and more dishes. 'I think it's going to be a long night.'

The smells from the food rise and stir my appetite, and I peer at the serving plates Uma brought in: *dahl*, and bowls of rice, *samosa*, *tandoori* chicken with a red sauce showered with pomegranate seeds.

I tuck in to the hot scrambled eggs. They are heavenly and slip down easily. Uma stands by my chair, hand on hip, watching as I devour the toast and slurp the lovely spiced tea.

I'm just about to fork the final bit of egg when I notice Nani looking my way. She's frowning, and when I follow her gaze it lands right on the ring.

Oh no! I forgot to take it off. I wriggle in my seat and clasp my fingers to hide the emerald, blood searing my cheeks.

'Who gave you that ring?' she asks, her voice sounding all fragile.

I open my mouth to answer but Sufia gets there first. 'She's been poking about in places she shouldn't,' she declares triumphantly. 'I found her in the old hut. She was literally lifting up the floorboards searching for stuff. That's where she found it.' Sufia looks so pleased with herself sitting there, arms crossed. She gives me another one of her shrivelling looks and bats her lashes.

'Didn't anyone tell you not to go there?' Nani's eyes spark and she sounds angry.

My stomach folds in on itself and I don't know what to do, so I stare at my plate and hide my hands under the table. I feel my lip tremble.

'And exactly what were *you* doing there, madam?' Aunt Simran asks Sufia, putting her fork down. '*You* know you're not allowed. I expect Tamarind just stumbled on it.'

'That's just typical,' cries Sufia, banging a fist on the table.

Nani has tears in her eyes. 'And if you were nice to Tamarind, maybe you would have told her that we don't go there any more, because after all, she didn't know.' She pauses and twists her hands together.

Arjun and me share a swift look. We can both sense where this is going.

'You're grounded,' says Aunt Simran.

'Again,' says Arjun under his breath.

Sufia's face is like a stone statue. She juts her chin and scrapes her chair across the wooden floor. 'Well, I might as well go to my room right now then . . . but

131

no, I can't go to *my* room because the *lovely* Tamarind is in there.'

'Upstairs, now!' Aunt Simran begins to stand up.

'I'm going, I'm going. Anyway, it's clear you prefer Tamarind and would rather have *her* as your daughter.' She gathers her bruised anger and hurls her final blow. 'I . . . I bet you wish you could get rid of me.'

20

'Stop. That's enough now,' continues Aunt Simran, her cheeks turning bright. 'I'll speak to you later.'

'And when your papa gets home,' adds Nani, 'he will speak to you as well.'

Sufia rushes out of the room and thunders up the stairs, thumping each step loudly with her feet.

Everyone returns to their food, but it's so quiet you can hear the spoons tapping the sides of the bowls as they carry on eating.

When the meal is finished and Aunt Simran starts clearing the dishes, Nani walks slowly round the table and holds my hand. 'We gave this ring to Chinty for her twelfth birthday. It's a very rare emerald that your *babajee* and Chinty found and he had it set into the silver star. I never saw it after she died, though. I thought it was lost for ever. Chinty used to love pretending she was the goddess Ishtar, pretending that the ring had magical powers. She imagined it could lead the way to treasure and secrets, glowing like a torch in the night.'

I take the ring off and hold it out to Nani. 'I'm sorry.' The clutch of tears slide down my cheeks. 'I shouldn't have gone in the hut.' The scrunched-up feelings cry themselves free, and I can't stop them now. 'I know I shouldn't have gone – Arjun warned me, but I was upset, and I ran into the wild garden and found it. There was a little monkey who came and he showed me the loose floorboard and the box inside the gap. There were other things too.'

Nani's face shadows with emotion again.

'A golden arrow with a white glittery feather on the end, some dried-up face paints – and the ring.' The tears fall even faster. 'It's the only proper thing I've ever had of Mum's a . . . and I'm so happy I found it. Sorry, Nani. I didn't mean to upset you.'

'I remember helping Chinty to decorate the box with pretty paper. It's where she kept all her special things.' Nani puts the ring back on my finger. 'Look how it fits you . . . I wish we could keep you for ever, Tamarind.' Her face begins to crumple. 'But your papa will be taking you away again, before we've even got to know you.'

*

Later in bed I'm tossing and turning. Outside, the rain is pulsing right under the shutters and lashing against the window panes. I'm desperate to see Ishta again, but there's no chance tonight. Thunder cracks, shaking the house as if it's wrapping monster arms around us.

My heart is racing and I yank the covers over my head, burying deep under the bedclothes, but even in here I can see the room light up as the lightning flashes, serpent-like, lashing the walls with its electric tongue.

Even though the storm is terrifying, I peel back the covers, sit up in bed and check my watch. It's only one thirty in the morning, there's still time to go into the garden if the storm finally breaks. How much longer is it going to go on?

A light appears under the door gap and careful footsteps tap-tap across the landing. It must be Arjun. The storm's probably frightened him.

I jump on to the cold floor and twist open the door, ready to invite him in, but it's not Arjun.

Sufia is creeping through the landing, a bulging rucksack on her back. Another flash of lightning startles her and she spots me in the doorway.

She steps into my room, and pulls the door closed behind her. 'Shhh!!'

'What are you doing?'

'What does it matter to you?' she spits. Her eyes

are red and I can tell she's been crying. 'Ever since Auntie Chinty died, nothing's been the same for me here. They sent me away to school to get rid of me when all I wanted to do was stay where all the memories were.'

I think she's going to soften and I start to feel sorry for her but then she starts her attack again. 'And now that *you're* here, everyone can't stop fussing over you. Tamarind this, Tamarind that! And I have to give up my room, Auntie Chinty's room . . . So anyway, since everyone prefers you, I'm leaving.'

'Where will you go? There's nowhere for miles.'

'Don't worry about me, I know the mountains around here, I'll be just fine. And don't you *dare* tell anyone where I've gone!'

She swivels round and carries on down the stairs, the storm still whirling furiously around the house. I run after her but she's already disappeared through the hall, clicking the front door closed.

I stand in the sombre hallway, the pale flames on the candles lining the sideboard wavering in the draughts. I hurry back to my room, heart thumping, and throw myself on the bed. I shut my eyes and bury myself deep under the covers. Let her go, what do I care! Even when I think she's going to be a bit kinder she just bites back. Outside, the wind is as wild and frantic as a pack of hungry wolves, lashing at the trees and hurling itself against the shutters. Instead of calming down, the storm is getting worse.

I imagine the family waking up to find Sufia missing, lost in the storm. As well as being angry with her they'll be so scared. The shutters bang furiously and thunder crashes so loudly I can feel its vibrations through my whole body. Even though I don't like Sufia, this family is still so broken even years after Mum's death. I can't let them lose Sufia as well.

I struggle into my thickest sweatshirt, pull the waterproof jacket Dad insisted I bring over my head, and put my tracksuit bottoms on. Sufia can't have got far. I'll find her and bring her back, stop her getting herself deeper into trouble and maybe, just maybe, she'll thank me for it.

I grab my torch and head downstairs. When I open the front door, the wind snatches it from my hands and I struggle to close it behind myself, but I push my body hard against it until it slams shut. No one will notice the bang over the noise of the storm.

The garden is wrecked. There are branches strewn over the lawns, leaves mounded in piles along the hedges, debris flying and swirling through the air. My heart pumps as I shield my eyes and run into the battering wind.

21

I hold my ring ahead of me, its emerald light glowing in the darkness – miraculously, the stars are breaking through. 'Show me the way,' I breathe. 'Where did she go?' An energy surges inside me and I chase after the light of the ring.

The rain has paused a moment, but lightning still flashes over the towering mountains and the thunder booms louder with each new clap. I wish I'd followed Sufia sooner.

I stare up at the stars, shining brighter than ever between the bruised purple clouds of the stormy sky. I sense a spark, travelling down from the universe, like the feeling you get when you walk between ancient standing stones at night. They're telling me to go on and find Sufia, that it's up to me, I'm Tamarind the brave! On instinct, I hold out my hand. My mum's ring is glowing with its clear green light, a single beam pointing towards the copse . . . towards the hut! Maybe Sufia is hiding there, waiting out the storm after all. I plunge further into the garden, following the light.

Water from the soaked branches drenches me as I run through the grasses and waist-high nettles now battered flat by the rain, past the rock, through the billowing branches of the trees in the copse and pause to catch my breath by the hut. No light shines in the windows. I stand on tiptoe, wipe the window clear of cobwebs and peer into the little hut, but it's empty. And the ring's beam is veering off now, towards the wild garden.

A strike of lightning illuminates the statue as I rush under the arch, into the wilderness of the tangled garden, and the rain begins again in torrents. I look about, blinking away the water streaming down my eyes and nose. I can't see Sufia anywhere. The clouds cover the stars and the ring seems to lose its glow; the beam of light that was so strong before is now weak and diffused.

I raise my hands, cup them to my mouth. 'Sufiiiia,' I call through the noise of the angry storm.

Nothing.

I run even further into the wild garden until the stitch in my side is howling, looking for any sign of where she might have gone. What if she's left the garden and ventured into the real wilderness of the Himalaya? Arjun said there were animals in the mountains – dangerous ones like tigers, snow leopards and packs of hungry wolves, like the ones that Ishta showed me through the gap in the hedge. Fear grips me as I imagine Sufia, headstrong and foolish, running away into the wild, too angry to think straight.

What if something terrible happens to her and I could have stopped it? I keep moving, fear shooting up my spine, sweat and rain trickling down my neck. I find the gap in the hedge at the furthest end of the garden, the one that Ishta wanted me to crawl through, where we saw the wolves – the one I was too scared to go through last time.

On hands and knees, I crawl along the slippery sodden ground and scramble through, the thorned branches ripping at my clothes, until I'm out the other side. The rain falls faster, icy drops hailing from above like liquid silver; down it pours, making rivers of the mud-clogged ground.

The storm shows no sign of relenting and I struggle against the wind and climb to higher ground, searching the shield of water that's everywhere. The rowing boat is still tied on the near edge of the dark churned-up lake, frantically dipping and jerking against the water. Is it better that she's on foot, or worse?

And then I hear a strange cry, carried on the wind. It's faint and far off, a deep-throated animal sound.

A bolt of panic shivers through my veins, and even though terror is ripping at my insides, I keep going, skirting the lake, dragging my feet through the wet earth, through the wild landscape, heading for the far side, towards the haunting noise. They can't blame me for anything if they know I did everything I could to save Sufia, that I risked my own life.

Thunder crashing, storm wailing, I sprint as fast as I can towards the arc of mountains before me. The ground is slippery and I splash my way onwards through earth-coloured puddles, the animal wail guiding me higher. I hold my ring ahead of me, praying for the clouds to shift and let its beam show me where to look, but the light is so dull now, the green glow of the emerald faded almost to nothing.

But the howling is getting louder; even in the clamour of the storm, I can hear the cries rising and rising, turning more frantic.

Through the veil of rain I see a dark hollow in the mountain ahead, a cave maybe, and my heart gives a skip. Perhaps Sufia is taking shelter there? But as I get

141

closer, the howling booms against the hard surface of the rock.

Wolves!

They're standing in front of the gaping cave, heads thrown back, white fur glistening, teeth bared, as if they're guarding something. They rise up in a fearful semicircle, howling at something inside the cave.

I duck behind a rock, straining my eyes for a sight of Sufia, and then I see her through the sheets of slate-grey rain – a huddled shape, crouched a little way into the cave. She has a torch in her hand and shines it at the wolves, protecting herself. She's built a small fire at the mouth of the cave, but still the wolves howl and agitate, stalking up and down.

'Sufia!' I call. 'Sufia, it's me, Tamarind! I'm going to help you.' She doesn't seem to hear me – and I've no idea what to do. My chest is tight, fear stretching the skin taut on my face, but I crawl nearer, licking salty sweat from my lips.

Crouching low like an animal, I hunker close to the ground, hoping my dark coat will camouflage me from the pack. But I know the wolves will catch my scent – they probably already know I'm here and the knowledge sends terror skittering through me.

I pause to gather my courage and advance, trembling, towards the entrance. The wolves are horribly close, their eyes fixed on Sufia, and finally she catches sight of me, her shocked eyes opening wider. 'Tamarind! Get away! It's too dangerous!'

Panic roots my feet to the ground as a few of the wolves slowly turn towards me. How am I going to help? I'm only a girl – and now I feel the danger so sharply it swamps me and I stagger backwards, my body telling me to run, but my feet clumsy and frozen with fear.

I fall, my clothes squelching in the mud as the wolves growl and spring towards me, lowering their heads to the rocks, looming closer, their meaty breath blooming the air.

'Run!' Sufia screams.

Her fire is sputtering as the wind and rain lash the opening of the cave. Once it goes out, she'll be defenceless.

We're *both* defenceless. The wolves' teeth shine in the night.

That's when the clouds part. Suddenly a confidence fills me up – a sense of purpose and light – and I know I'm *meant* to be here. I can do it! I lift the ring and it glows weakly before suddenly casting a bright beam across the sky.

The wolves turn and, as if confused, stay grounded to the spot as their eyes latch on to the ring's magical glow.

Another voice calls over the storm. 'Tamarind. Up here!'

I shift my gaze to a ledge above the cave. It's Ishta! The wind buffets her so violently that she's struggling to even stand – she's flickering, appearing and disappearing along with the ring's light as the clouds race across the stars. I squint, certain my eyes are deceiving me. How is that possible?

She draws an arrow and holds it tight against the bow in front of her, pulls her arm back with confidence and whips the arrow high above the circle of wolves. The arrow glints bronze, forging a straight line into the storm-crazed sky. The wolves follow its track, obviously spooked, howls thronging the air as their attention is distracted from Sufia and me.

A sudden crashing of thunder and lightning bombs above us, confusing the wolves even more. 'Run, Sufia,' I shout. 'Come on!'

She leaps to her feet and runs from the cave, darts her eyes across to where Ishta stands on the ledge, poised, ready with another arrow. But Sufia's eyes slide over Ishta as if there's nothing there. She grabs my hand. 'Come on, Tam!' She tugs me back towards the garden as the rain pelts down on us both.

I glance over my shoulder as I allow myself to be

pulled along – there's no sign now of Ishta on the ledge over the cave. Where did she go?

Below, the wolves snarl their finely carved fangs and rush into the cave, sending a howl into the storm so fierce and strong it carries on the wind like a heart-rending lament. Whatever's in there, they're more interested in it than in us.

But what about Ishta? She saved us and she's still out here, in danger. I stop and pull my hand away from Sufia's.

'Ishta!' I shout. 'Where are you?'

But she's gone.

'Who are you shouting at?' Sufia says wildly, tugging my arm. 'Don't look back – just keep running!'

I feel a heart-pang of sadness and grasp Sufia's hand. Together we hurtle down the slope. We tighten our grip to save each other from slipping on the muddy ground and struggle away from the cave, further and further towards the garden, panting hard as the gusts of wind pluck at our clothes, our hair, our faces and the rain lashes us again and again.

22

When at last I can't run any more and we're nearly back by the gap in the hedge, I try to slow my breathing and stare frantically into the distance, back towards the mountains and the cave, searching for any sign of Ishta.

'I'm so sorry,' Sufia stutters, softer rain now mixing with the tears that slide down her cheeks. We tramp along the side of the lake towards the garden.

I don't know what to say so I just squeeze her hand tighter.

'Everyone was so cross with me,' she sobs. 'I thought it was better if I just left.' Her clothes are torn and plastered to her body.

'Did the wolves attack you?'

'No. I took shelter in the cave when the storm got too wild for me to go on – I could barely see my hand in front of my face. I was scared but I didn't see the cubs in there until I lit the fire, and then the wolves appeared at the entrance . . . I'm so stupid, I just didn't think.' Sufia's face is ashen. 'They just wanted to be with their cubs.'

I put an arm around her shoulder and she doesn't shrug it away. It surprises me. I leave it there for a moment before dropping it to my side. I'm still not sure how Sufia feels about me, but – after all that – it seems she's finally beginning to soften towards me.

So maybe I should trust her.

I swallow, shield my eyes from the rain. 'Did . . . didn't you see the girl, on the ledge?' I ask.

Sufia shakes her head. 'I couldn't see anyone.'

I blink. I don't understand how that's possible. 'What about the arrow she fired across the sky? She saved us.'

Sufia frowns. 'I saw lightning, Tamarind. It was so bright it distracted the wolves. And then the thunder. I . . . don't think there can have been anyone up there.' She gazes at me closely as we reach the boundary.

'No, I'm sure she was there. I know her. It was a girl I met in the garden earlier this week . . . Ishta,' I say, between breaths. 'We made friends, really good friends. She lives around here but I didn't know she could shoot an arrow like that.'

Sufia is staring, her eyes wide. 'Ishta? That's—'

'What?'

Sufia shakes her head. 'Never mind. Let's go, we need to get warm and dry – quickly.'

We limp together through the wild garden, under the stone arch and head towards the hut, the rain still falling, the storm still chasing at our heels.

When we get to the hut we stop, too weak and battered to take the final steps to the house.

'C-can we shelter here?' Sufia is shaking. 'I can't go any further.'

I scramble for the key in the pile of grass and push open the door, bundling us both inside. Sufia's breath is still beating out of her and she clings to my arm, her eyes wild.

We squirm out of our wet shoes and outer layers and leave them in a soggy pile on the floor. I pull at the duvet and with a final bit of strength lead Sufia to the bunk bed – to Mum's bed. She collapses, falling against the pillow, and draws the covers around herself, her teeth chattering, her hair wet. I tumble in next to her and feel her feet, blocks of damp ice, touching mine. I pull one of the other duvets on top of the first one to warm us up quicker.

'The girl on the ledge . . .' says Sufia as if she's

delirious, staring into space. 'Ishta. She sent the lightning to save us?'

'Sufia . . . it was an arrow, not lightning.' I tuck her in, feeling like the grown-up of the two of us, even though she's six years older. 'You've had a real shock, that's all. I met Ishta a few times and she's definitely real. She's a real person, just like you and me. We played together and she showed me the gap in the hedge. That's how she got into the garden and how I knew how to get out.' I frown. 'She saved us, though, that's for sure. I just hope she's OK.'

Now that we're both safe, I feel my energy fading. Blood rushes to my frozen fingers and toes, blazes my cheeks.

The rain continues to pour, drumming on the roof of the hut, the storm thrashing against the small windows.

Sufia lies very still, her eyes shut – but she's warming up, and I am too. I touch her pale forehead and she stirs, giving a deep sigh, falling into sleep.

My stomach knots as I think of Ishta out there in the storm, and I touch my ring, asking for the emerald's light to find her and keep her safe.

23

When I open my eyes in the morning, I'm surrounded by a halo of faces peering over the bed. I blink the sleep away, confused about where I am and what's going on. The rain is still tapping at the window and flurries of wind whip stray branches against the roof.

It's Nani and Arjun, and I quickly remember why I'm sleeping in the forbidden hut with Sufia still snoring at my side.

'Are you OK?' asks Arjun. 'We looked all over for you.'

'I'm sorry, Nani,' I begin, my throat like sandpaper, bracing myself to take the flak.

She shushes me, and Arjun runs outside, shouting that we've been found.

Nani perches on the edge of the bed and looks around, puts her warm hands on my head and kisses my hair. 'Chinty always adored coming here,' she sighs, looking about the hut, brushing away the tears that slide down her cheeks.

'Don't cry, Nani,' I say, holding her hand tight.

Her gaze falls on to the ring. 'I know we can't change the past,' she continues. 'And maybe now that you're here, I can start to let go . . . Chinty would love you to enjoy the hut, and I'm so pleased that Sufia has finally made friends with you.' Nani strokes Sufia's sleeping face.

I leap under the bed and bring out the patterned cardboard box with Mum's things in it. 'This is where I found the ring, Nani.' I open the lid and show her the wooden arrow painted gold with the white feather on the tip and the face paints.

Nani's breath catches as she stares at the childhood treasures. 'Chinty loved dressing up, she was always pretending to be a warrior or an explorer – always something adventurous.' She smiles. 'I want you to have this box. Will you keep her things safe, Tamarind?'

My heart leaps and I clutch the box, a smile beaming across my face. 'Of course. Thank you, Nani.'

Sufia begins to stir as Arjun returns to the hut with Aunt Simran. Sufia sits up slowly, rubbing at her eyes.

'What were you thinking?' begins Aunt Simran, her brows knotted with worry. 'Going out in that storm.'

'I . . . it was me, Aunt Simran,' I blurt, Sufia and I exchanging a fleeting look. 'I wanted to sleep in the hut one last time, in case the storm made it impossible later . . . to feel close to Mum. Sufia was worried about me and followed me out.'

Aunt Simran's expression softens and she gathers the covers off us. 'Well then . . . let's get you both back to the house and warm.'

After stuffing a couple of pistachio pastries down with glugs of hot milk, me and Sufia are sent upstairs to the bedroom, 'to rest'. We get into clean pyjamas, socks and thick jumpers and dive into the covers.

'I'm sorry I've been so mean to you,' says Sufia. 'You won't tell anyone what happened, will you?'

'Of course I won't.'

'Thank you for coming to find me,' she sniffs. 'It was such a stupid thing to do, to go out into the storm.'

'It's OK,' I say quietly.

'We have more in common than you think,' she says, her jaw tensing. 'I . . . wasn't always in this family.' She seems to struggle with the words. 'I-I came to live here when I was two years old. Before that I lived in an orphanage. My parents, I mean my *real* parents, were killed in an earthquake that hit the Himalaya.' She lets the tears come and they fall on to the bed.

I put my arm around her shoulder again and this time keep it there for longer, feeling her body shaking with grief.

'It's not like they make me feel like an outsider. I know they love me, I get everything and more, but sometimes I don't know where I belong.'

'I know how hard *that* can be,' I say. 'I'm really sorry, Sufia. You must miss your parents too, just like I miss Mum, even though you don't remember them.'

She lifts a gold chain from underneath her jumper and shows me a small locket. 'This is the only photo I have of them. Mum told me the houseparents gave it to them along with a pair of green knitted bootees, when they adopted me from the orphanage.'

I remember the bootees and how angry Sufia was when I knocked them off the shelf, and now I understand why.

24

We sit side by side on the bed, the duvet over our legs, as Sufia shows me her locket. The locket is scratched and tarnished with age. The metal edge closest to the opening is worn from being held. 'Your parents look really kind and lovely.'

Sufia smiles. 'When I was little, Auntie Chinty made such a fuss over me. She painted my nursery, read me stories – made me feel safe. You see, Mum told me it was Auntie Chinty's idea to adopt me, after the news of the earthquake. It wasn't so far from here, she saw my photo in the papers and Mum said she fell in love with me.'

Before today I would have felt a pang of jealousy that Sufia got to do all those things with Mum, but I push the feelings away.

'She would have done the same for you,' says

Sufia. 'She adored you. I know the family think she was a bit wild, but for me she was the best.'

'And that's what *we* have in common, we both loved Chinty,' I say.

Sufia gives me a big hug. 'And love is stronger than blood.' She looks at Mum's ring in a strange way and I think maybe she's going to ask if she can try it. 'Tamarind.' She's starting to sound agitated and keeps staring at the ring. 'I started to tell you last night . . . you thought I was imagining things because of the fright and being in the storm. You know the girl you saw?'

'You mean Ishta? I already told you.' I'm feeling a little frustrated now. I know what I saw! 'You have to believe me that she's real!'

Sufia holds me by the shoulders. 'Tamarind, I believe you. But please . . . tell me everything about her. What did you do together? You said you . . . played?'

And so I tell her. About Hanu the monkey and the swing. About how we could meet only at night and even then, only when the sky was clear. How she gave me the seed pod – I slip it out of my pocket to show her – and I gave her my badge in return. How she told me, once, that she longed to explore but couldn't leave. How despite this, she said that one day she wouldn't be there and that I should remember she was always my friend.

At last Sufia sighs. 'Listen to me. If you're so sure you saw a girl, dressed like that and calling herself Ishta . . . a girl who disappeared . . . I think it could have been Auntie Chinty.'

'How can that be possible?' I ask, my heart pumping. 'Are . . . are you saying that you think the girl Ishta is really my *mum*?'

'I don't *know* what I'm saying,' says Sufia; her cheeks look hot. 'I'm just as confused as you, but the description matches, and Ishta is what Chinty always used to call herself when she played. And *nobody* else lives around here. She even had a little monkey friend – she would slip him bits of food when I was little. But after she died, he returned to the wild.' She sniffs, a tear wobbling down her cheek. 'All the things she said to you, about this being her home and not being able to leave . . . all of it makes sense.' She sits up and lifts the long seed pod from the table. 'And this . . . this is a tamarind seed. From the tree with the swing.'

I blink and sit up next to her. 'That's a tamarind tree?'

'Yes. It was your mum's favourite tree,' says Sufia, pressing the seed into my palm. 'You were named

156

after it, Tam. Now do you see why I think Ishta *is* Chinty?'

Just when things were settling down, the questions are getting even bigger and I don't know what to think any more. I try to get my thoughts in order but they keep fluttering off in all directions. 'So . . . so you think she's – like a ghost?'

'People's spirits sometimes stay around,' says Sufia. 'At least that's what Uma says.'

'She didn't seem like a ghost.' I wipe my slippery palms on the covers. 'We played together. On the swing. She felt real.'

'Maybe . . . maybe she wanted to meet you. Just like you were trying to get close to her, she was trying to get close to you too. And perhaps, all this time, she's been waiting for you to come home.'

A tingle spreads through my body, like something from a dream or memory is trying to knock at my mind, make me take notice, and I wish I'd paid more attention in the garden when me and Ishta first met.

'Maybe she couldn't leave,' says Sufia, 'until you came back.'

'If it *was* Mum, why didn't she tell me? She could have told me everything.' It's my turn to get agitated now, and I feel my stomach tying into knots. 'Why did she pretend her name was Ishta?'

Sufia shrugs. 'I don't know. Maybe she didn't want to frighten you. She wanted to get to know you for real – that wouldn't have happened if you realized the truth. And as for the name Ishta . . .' She looks thoughtful. 'Like I said, she loved to act out scenes from the goddess Ishtar's life when she was a child – so there's that. And then there's the idea of Ishta – it means "favourite" or "cherished". I wonder if she was hoping you would cherish her.'

'None of this makes sense, Sufia.' My head is full of bizarre thoughts and I don't know what's real any more. I shake my head. 'As soon as I can, I'm going back to the garden to find her. I'll prove to you that she *does* live around here somewhere and she can tell you herself.'

I fling open the bedroom door and lead Sufia downstairs, desperate to get to the garden, but everyone is milling about and Aunt Simran won't let us out of her sight. Disappointment hammers my chest as I realize I can't get past Chacha Dev, who is all over the garden with Kamaal clearing up the debris and the falling branches.

Every time Sufia or I look like we're heading off somewhere, Aunt Simran seems to find some small task for us to do – it's just not going to be possible today.

Once dinner is over, Nani insists we go to bed early, after last night's excitement, and even *I* know that sneaking out after dark tonight would be really stupid – and they'd worry so much if they found me missing again. Lying in bed, my mind is alight with a plan – I only have one day left . . .

25

It's Saturday. My last chance. After breakfast, I throw on some clothes, fish clean trainers from my case, tie the laces as quickly as I can and sneak out of the room, Sufia following me.

Through the dining room I spy Chacha Dev on the verandah lifting the shutters. The storm is finally over, but out in the garden branches and leaves are still all over the lawn.

Sufia catches me and tugs at my arm before I reach the verandah. She leads me through a door. 'I think they'll go really crazy if they see us going out again – this is a sly way out.'

We wind past the kitchen, through the other end of the house and make our way hurriedly out of a side entrance, along the brick wall of the orchard where the unsettled clucking of the chickens rises into the morning air.

As we sneak over the nettles to the wild garden, I glance up at the statue above the arch. My heart won't stop banging and butterflies whir around my stomach, bringing the rushed breakfast up to my mouth, but I race forward, desperate to see Ishta, hoping she'll be there swinging high through the branches of the beautiful tree. The *tamarind* tree.

My fists are tight balls as we hurry to the right of the garden, picking our way over fallen branches and long strands of leaves until the tree appears ahead of us, and my heart feels like it's stopped.

'It's been struck by lightning,' I cry, my chest tightening. I'm racing towards it, ahead of Sufia, my legs pumping hard.

The branches of the tree are charred, the trunk a blackened pillar – at its base a pile of ghostly ashes, leaves strewn under its spiky canopy, destroyed. The swing is broken and twisted on the ground nearby.

'Ishta!' I cry. 'Where are you?'

I hunt further into the garden, searching between the tangled trees for signs of her, calling her name. But there's nothing, only my strangled voice. The storm has torn everything to pieces.

Sufia's hand curls into mine.

I place my palms flat against the charred trunk of the tamarind tree, all its beauty burned away, and feel a knot flaming my throat. This was my tree – mine and Mum's tree – and I didn't even know it.

The smell of charcoal and dampness rests on the branches instead of the scents of the leaves that unfurled into the wind before. I feel the loss deep inside, in the small heart-shaped space under my rib.

'If I'd known this was my special tree I would have been down here all the time,' I say softly.

'I'm sorry,' says Sufia, staring at the ground. 'We're all so used to not talking about Auntie Chinty. It's stupid.' She lifts her chin. 'All of us need to figure out how to start remembering.' She kicks at the fallen branches under the tree.

Sadness settles like a dull ache in my chest. I search the ground for flecks of gold dust, peer into the distance for a sign of Hanu's glitter trail, but there's nothing.

'You have to decide what you believe for yourself,' Sufia adds.

I remember what Uma said before about how the house and gardens were different since I arrived, how I'd woken something up. Or someone. I peer at my ring, the emerald sparkling in the sunshine. 'I'm just not sure. How can it be possible?'

Sufia has deep circles around her eyes and still looks shaken from the night before. 'I don't know,' she says. 'It sounds crazy to me too.'

'Let's go back,' I say, taking her by the arm. Even though she's way older than me and taller, she lets me guide her back through the garden.

When we arrive at the hut, I spy Chacha Dev cutting back the nettles. The door is wide open and Nani has a broom and is sweeping up the leaves and twigs that scooted under the gap. She smiles at us. 'We're going to freshen things up, maybe even paint it, so you can all enjoy it, like Chinty did. I brought some old family albums down. I thought you'd like to see some photos, Tamarind.'

Sufia's eyes are wide. 'Really?' she says breathlessly.

'I think I'm ready now – it's time,' says Nani, heaving a sigh. 'Now come and sit on the bed and we'll look at them together.'

My heart lurches and I steady myself as I sit between Nani and Sufia on one of the freshly made beds, the blank spaces in my memory ready to be filled at last.

The first few pages are baby shots that look a bit like the ones of me that Dad has on the shelves at home.

'That's Chinty as a baby,' says Nani. 'See how similar you look?'

I feel a swell of pride to think that I look like Mum.

Sufia shuffles closer. 'She was really cute.'

'And look at this one.'

I freeze. Mum's wearing an embroidered flowery dress, a sheepskin waistcoat, baggy trousers, and has a bow slung across her chest. She's holding up an arrow as if she's getting ready to fire, and her hair is twisted over the top of her head.

It's Ishta. I feel my eyes sting with tears as I stare at the photo, trying to work out what I believe. Now there's no doubt in my mind: Ishta and Mum are one and the same. Sufia was right. I glance up, catch her eye and nod.

Nani laughs. 'I think we've got that outfit some-where in the house, in the playroom in the tower, I expect. She loved her book about Ishtar, and after that she wanted to dress like this all the time.'

My heart is racing and I want to ask Nani if she believes in ghosts and if she thinks that everything has changed since I arrived, like Uma said: if she thinks that I've woken Mum's spirit . . . But I stay quiet because I'm sure it would be too much for her to take, just as she's letting go of the past and moving forward.

We stay a while longer in the hut, looking through the album, Nani and Sufia chatting about the happy times in the past while I listen. Finally I'm gaining a sense of who Mum was and how I'm like her, and listening to the stories brings a big smile to my face.

Nani shows me photos of Mum when she was fat with her baby bump, sitting on the verandah looking happy, and it makes me feel like I belong here – like I always belonged here. I have two homes now.

Nani looks more relaxed than I've seen her, as if she can enjoy the memories at last without feeling sad.

Later, once everyone is asleep and the house is quiet, I get dressed. Dad will be here tomorrow and I have to go on my own to the garden one final time to find Ishta – I need to tell her I know who she really is, that I love her and miss her. My insides are knotted with desperation – if only I'd realized sooner that Ishta was my mum, I would have asked her so many questions and told her everything about me.

Sufia doesn't stir as I tiptoe past her bed – she's sleeping in Chinty's old room with me now – click the door open and leave the room. The route through the house is familiar and I speed silently down the stairs, across the hallway and into the indigo softness of the Himalayan night.

The bright yellow moon sits high above the tower-ing mountains and I touch my sparkling ring, holding it ahead of me like I did before, hoping it will bring me to Mum. But the ring doesn't shine as clear as it did before – the light is dispersed, scattered all around me. My chest tightens with worry.

As I approach the statue and hurry under the arch, there's still no sign of Ishta. I feel a patter of nerves rattle through my chest and I fix on the ring, the star of Ishta, spreading its light into the darkness.

I head straight for the tamarind tree, tramping through the damp wilderness until I see it ahead of me. In the night it looks even more desolate, its jagged branches sharp against the moonlight.

'Ishta,' I cry. 'Ishta, it's me – Tamarind.' I search everywhere. 'Mum! Where are you?'

But there's no answer, only the gentle wind rustling the grasses, cooling my red cheeks.

I throw myself on to the hard ground. 'Why won't you come, Mum? Now that I know it's you. I could tell you all about myself, and we could be friends, *real* friends.' My breath shudders from deep inside me and I let the damp earth muffle the sobs, the night air ruffling at my hair. I bang the ground with my fists, as if Mum will hear me knocking and come running. But nothing.

Until a soft patter of feet makes me sit up and listen.

'Hanu,' I pant, trying to control my sobs. 'It's you.'

He uncurls my fists with his slender fingers, opens my palm and slips a soft hand in. Then he flicks his tail and gold dust lights up the dark night as he lets go of my hand and races under the tree, climbs the charred branches and howls, beating his chest like a drum.

'Where is she, Hanu?' Tears slide from the corners of my eyes.

He rushes back down, leaps on to my hip and I just manage to catch him. He rests his head in the nook of my shoulder and chin, wiping at my cheeks. I feel the pulse of his tiny heartbeat.

I let the scrunched-up feelings free, swallow hard. 'She's gone, hasn't she?'

26

'*We'll call you Tamarind,*' she sings. '*Tamarind, like my beautiful tree . . . I'll rock you in the tamarind tree . . .*'

'Tam, Tamarind! Wake up.'

'Mum?' I blink open my eyes. The familiar tune clinging to my dreams, like it's always been there, just a heartbeat away.

Sufia is shaking me. 'Happy birthday!' She's holding a small tray with a cupcake in the centre and tea lights all around it.

I rub my eyes and sit up slowly.

'They're already cooking downstairs, sweeping, cleaning. It's mayhem.'

I touch my ring. 'I was dreaming of Mum. It was almost daylight and the tree was in blossom and Mum was there, swinging in the tree and she said she loved me.'

'Of course she loved you.' Sufia squeezes in next to me. 'You don't have to worry about anything now. Relax and enjoy your birthday.' She holds the cupcake towards me. 'Blow out the candles.'

'OK, bossy,' I laugh, taking a bite of the cake.

She leans on to the floor and picks up a rectangular package. 'This is for you.'

I tear the patterned paper, and carefully untie the ribbon. 'I put an album together for you. It's got lots of old family photos, ones of your mum when she was little and Babajee too.'

I hold the album to my chest. 'Thank you, Sufia. This is the best present ever.' I open the first page, see a photo of Mum as a baby, and underneath a photo of me laying on the same patterned blanket.

It's like a jigsaw puzzle coming together; the more I find out, the clearer everything feels.

'Why didn't I realize that Ishta was my mum?' I don't want to cry on my birthday, but I just can't help it and I let the tears plop on to my lap.

'Look, don't cry,' Sufia says gently. 'It's incredible what happened, so special. You actually got to meet her.' Sufia puts an arm around my shoulder. 'It's not something that happens every day. Just think how lucky you are! You'll have those memories of meeting her and playing with her for ever.'

'You're right,' I sniff. 'Even though I didn't know she was my mum, I still got to spend time with her, right? And she was such fun.'

'Amazing, I'd say,' smiles Sufia. 'The way she saved me from the wolves, like she was keeping watch over us.' She looks down at my ring. 'Maybe she still is.'

Remembering my time in the magical wild garden and doing all those fun things together like real friends makes me feel better.

'And I know you've only got today but there's still time to ask Nanijee whatever you want, and you *did* get to sleep in her room, and in the hut where she used to play. *And* it's your birthday!' Sufia stands up. 'Come on, you'd better get up! Your dad and Chloe will be here soon and there's loads to do.'

'OK.' I tuck the album under the bed covers and quickly change.

'And just as we made friends,' Sufia twiddles her ponytail, 'you're leaving.'

'It doesn't have to stop, does it? I'll come back next summer and maybe you can come to England. I don't think we'll find a secret garden but there are fun things to do. I can show you round Bristol – that's cool. And Sufia' – I look her in the eye – 'thank you for sharing your story with me.'

'Tamarind,' calls Nani, as we run through the hallway and into the dining room. The doors are wide open and it's a beautiful day. 'Come here.' She clasps my face between her palms and plants a kiss on my cheek. 'We have hardly seen you this week, running wild in the garden at all hours of the day and night.' She looks over to Uma who is tidying up. 'Now, I had a special outfit made for your birthday party. Try it on later – surprise your papa.'

Sufia and I exchange a glance. I give Nani a big hug. 'Thank you. I'm sure I'll love it.'

'I'm glad you two have made friends at last,' smiles Nani. 'We have to stick together.' She hugs both me and Sufia. 'It has been so good for me to have you here, Tamarind, you've helped me so much. Now I feel I can talk about Chinty and remember her again.' She smiles, looking at my star of Ishta ring. 'Can you help me with a few things? This is going to be a special mountain celebration, so let's show your dad and Chloe how we do it.' She sprinkles pomegranate seeds on to a platter of rice.

But although I try to get into the party spirit, I can't get the tamarind tree out of my mind. It makes me so sad to think of what happened to it. I walk out on to the verandah, leaving Sufia to help Nani. The sun is rising, the final traces of the storm fading.

171

Birds call to each other, diving and swooping through the sky.

The top of the tree is visible, the destroyed branches poking up like deadly fingers. But there's something different about it today . . .

I step into the garden and walk away from the house, my ring glowing and glinting in the morning sun. The breeze carrying a peppery scent blows over me, ruffles my hair.

It's like the wild garden is drawing me to it and I run over the mown grass, where the nettles used to be, past the rock and the hut, under the crumbling arch, past the goddess, same as ever with her beckoning hand.

By the time I reach the tamarind tree I'm out of breath, my cheeks hot. I stop suddenly under the boughs of its raven branches, blood pumping fast through my veins, amazement making my jaw drop.

How can it be? I couldn't see it properly from a distance but the craggy tree is in full blossom!

All along its stark branches, swirls of flowers burst into bloom. I touch the petals lower down, trying to see if it's my mind playing tricks, but they feel silky soft, like the freshest newest flowers opening on a spring day, real as anything under my fingertips.

I stand below the canopy, taking in the cloud of

flowers. The morning light shines through the froth of green-white petals bending on long, drooping stems and it takes my breath away. Their sweet peppery scent fills my nose, my head, my body, like I remember this moment, a sudden memory from long ago engraved for ever.

27

I wrap my arms as far round the blackened trunk as they will go and let my body soak in the smells of the flowers and the deep scent of warm earth, tilt my head and rest my forehead on its bark. I sink into the tree, giving myself up to my wild garden mother. I start to hear a familiar tune, carried on the breeze . . .

Tamarind.

My breath catches.

As I look up, half blinded by sunlight, I see a swing flying through the flowers, carrying a laughing young woman, her hair cut short, straight nose, high cheekbones. She's older than when she was Ishta and we met in the garden. But she's definitely my mum.

I'm trembling as I lift my ring in front of my face. It's glowing so bright now. And I can hear a singing voice, carried on the wind – the tune I heard when I arrived and before Ishta first appeared . . .

'*We'll call you Tamarind,*' she sings. '*Tamarind, like my beautiful tree . . . I'll rock you in the tamarind tree . . .*'

I remember how we flew through the air, the tangled garden below us, spying the very top of the house, its turrets poking into the blue sky, and how I was scared – and thrilled – and I didn't want it to end.

I lift my gaze again. Mum is swinging back and forth through the tree, waving her hand, rising into the blue, arcing through the branches. The higher she goes, the more she seems to fade.

'*Shall we go even higher, Tamarind?*'

I watch as she leaves the tree behind and rises into the lightening turquoise sky, her outline mingling with the mountains and the low clouds. I stay still, my hand over my eyes, squinting until I can't see her any more, only the faint moon and the morning star that always sits beside it, the first to appear and the last to leave. I feel my heart miss a beat, and look at my ring, its light beaming into the sky, following Mum.

'*Don't forget me.*' The song rises into the rose-blushed light.

For the first time I feel surrounded by an invisible

power, something far bigger than I've ever experienced before. I don't understand it but I give myself up to it, stare at the sky that makes a shield above us, shedding its hidden starlight from millions of years ago into this mysterious place, my home.

I know now that Mum will always be with me whatever happens. She's all around and everywhere, watching over me – the star of Ishta.

28

When I get back to the house, there's breakfast on the verandah. Arjun has been busy with his origami and is folding a new creature.

'Hi,' he says, frowning as I sit between him and Sufia. 'I've been meaning to ask you, how come you two are suddenly so chummy?' A look of confusion clouds his face.

'We finally found out that we actually have a lot in common,' I say, shifting closer. I lower my voice so only he can hear. 'I won't forget how you made me feel welcome, Arjun. That was really special and made all the difference – thank you. And I can't wait for you to visit Bristol so I can show you around.'

'Yes,' adds Sufia. 'Both of us. We're all like old friends now.'

Arjun gives me one of his warm smiles and rolls

his eyes at Sufia, like he'll never understand her, and carries on folding the paper.

Uma and Dev are primping everything up, dusting things and hanging up colourful bunting.

Uma leaves her chores for a moment and moves a platter closer to me. She scoops a big spoonful on to my plate. 'This is the one with less chilli in it.'

'What is it?' I ask.

'Kedgeree. All the things you like with an Indian twist. Rice, onion, cardamom and lentils.'

I take a mouthful. 'Not bad,' I smile.

'Look at you,' she says. 'I knew I'd get you to eat more than scrambled egg and toast. You've made me proud.' She pushes a small plate of *gulab jaman* towards me and I eat it whole, its sweetness filling my mouth with happiness.

'Thank you, Uma,' I say, touching her hand. 'Thank you for looking after me.'

Nani comes in from the dining room. 'When you've had enough, let's try your outfit on before your papa and Chloe arrive. And I have something else to show you.'

I eat quickly, then Nani takes my hand and together we climb the stairs. She pauses at the top and opens a cupboard, reaches up to the top shelf and brings down a small cotton bag. 'Let's go into your room. I put your *lehenga* in there.'

We go into the bedroom. Nani sits on the edge of the bed.

'You're going too soon,' she says. 'I've hardly had chance to see you.'

'I really want to come back . . . if you'll have me.'

'Don't talk silly nonsense – of course, we'll always have you.' She opens the bag. 'This was Chinty's baby bag for you. She came here just before you were born and she collected things for you. Look. These little socks, a silver rattle and this book of stories.'

'But why didn't I have it before?'

'Your papa took you away,' she says, looking suddenly agitated. 'Before we even had chance to get to know you properly.'

'But why, Nanijee?'

She twists her hands. 'We were so angry with them. They weren't married or *anything*.'

'Sufia said that Mum died so I could live. Is it true?' Salty tears drip into my mouth and this time, I don't try to stop them.

'Come here.' Nani dabs my cheeks with the edge of her soft shawl. 'Chinty didn't die because of you. Don't ever think that. I remember just after you were born, she was so proud, she loved you so much. But there were complications and . . . we lost her.'

'You really miss her, don't you?' I say, before I can stop myself.

It's Nani's turn to cry now. She swipes her face with the palm of her hand and puts her hands together in prayer. 'It wasn't to be.'

'Do you believe in magic?' I ask.

'In India there is magic all around, so yes I do.'

'What would you think if I said that this morning I saw Mum on a swing in the blossoming branches of the tamarind tree?'

'Did you really see that?' Nani cups my chin. She's kind, but I can tell she doesn't believe me. 'Your *babajee* made a swing for her when she was small, in the tamarind tree. When she was expecting, you used to wriggle around like crazy, hiccupping. Sitting on the swing used to settle you – that's why she called you Tamarind. It's so sad that the tree was struck by lightning.' She hugs me again. 'Try on your outfit, it's your birthday and we should think of happy things.' She lifts the *lehenga* from the bed.

I slip on the long green skirt with sparkles along the bottom and the short embroidered top.

'Sit on the floor, I'll plait your hair, like I used to when Chinty was your age.' She pushes her fingers through my tangled hair, smoothing it into two neat plaits. She finds some ribbon in the bag and threads it through the ends and finally makes a fancy style with the plaits over my head. 'There,' she smiles. 'That's how Chinty liked her hair done on dress-up days. Green was Chinty's colour too. You are so like her, Tamarind. It gives me such joy to see you. I mean that from the bottom of my heart.'

I hug Nani and she holds me tight.

'Now, I'd better go down and check on the preparations.'

'C-could I show you the tree, Nani? You can see for yourself, all the blossom came back.'

She hesitates and looks at the floor. 'OK,' she says. 'Let's go and take a look.'

We make our way slowly away from the house, through the neat gardens with their fresh flowers opening from new buds, until we see the hut. We walk under the stone arch and into the wild garden, the sun lighting the leaves and the gentle summer breeze flapping at Nani's shawl.

To my relief, the lightning-struck tree is still filled with blossom. I take Nani's hand and give it a squeeze. 'See, Nani!'

She doesn't speak, stays beside me, staring at the tree, as if she's trying to take everything in.

'Come on.' I lure her closer and we walk together under the canopy and touch the darkened trunk.

'It's amazing,' she says at last. 'Nearly as beautiful as before, and maybe in time the whole tree will grow. You know . . . When your mum was expecting you she got a real taste for *imilie* chutney.'

'The sour dark chutney that *I* like?'

'Yes. It's made from the fruits of this tree. *Imilie* means tamarind.'

I smile and take in the scent of the tree one final time, walking further until I feel like I'm part of the tree again.

And then I catch sight of something lying between the tree's great roots. 'Nani, look!'

29

On the ground, hidden among the fallen branches, lie a bow and an arrow. I slowly pick them up, feel an electric charge pump down my arm. The bow curves gracefully, and when I run my finger along the length of the silver string it gives off a resonating soulful sound. It's the bow she used to frighten off the wolves and I'm convinced that Mum left it for me, a parting gift from her.

Nani stares at the bow, a frown appearing between her brows. She leans against me, steadying herself, looking more closely at it.

'Look, Nani, it says *C.K.S.G.* – Mum's name, *Chinty Kaur Sher-Gil*. It's engraved along the top.'

'How strange . . . it's been so long since I saw Chinty's bow and here it is in the garden, and look how shiny it is, like it's been looked after and cared for.' After the initial shock, Nani doesn't seem upset by it. 'She loved archery,' she says, her voice dreamy.

'Nani,' I begin. 'Would you mind if I kept it? I might become an archer like Mum.'

'Of course you should have it.'

We stand under the tamarind tree one final time, the breeze billowing through the blossom, Nani hugging me close.

'We should get back,' she says finally. 'Our guests will be arriving and I expect you're looking forward to seeing your papa again.'

When we get back to the house, things are ready for the party; the table on the verandah is set with flowers and dotted with tea lights and all the bunting is swaying softly. I give Nani a final hug and run up to my room to put the bow and arrow away.

I sit on the bed, the bow and arrow resting in my hands, and I hope Aunt Simran won't be rude to Dad like she was at the airport. I want so badly to make this family whole again – and Dad is the final piece of this puzzle.

There's a loud beep outside the window – a car horn! I leave the bow and arrow on the bed, rush over and lift the curtain to catch the big people carrier swooping towards the house. 'It's Dad!' I hurry on to the landing and, holding up my swishy skirt, sprint down the stairs and out the front door.

The door to the car slides open as I take the steps two at a time and crash into Dad, wrapping my arms around him as he springs out of the car.

'Whoa. Happy birthday,' he laughs, lifting me into the air. 'And who are you? Where's my little Bristol girl?'

'Dad!' I snuggle my face into his chest and feel everything relax.

'I missed you,' he says, breathing into the top of my head.

'Me too.'

'But you've had fun?'

'It's been amazing, Dad.'

'Looks like you've been getting totally into the India vibe too. Great outfit.'

'Hi, Tam.' It's Chloe, beaming behind Dad.

'Hi, Chloe.' I give her a proper hug. I want to make her feel welcome. 'Did you have a good honeymoon?'

She exchanges a look with Dad and smiles. 'Yes, we did. Thank you, Tam. You look . . . different. Happy, lovely. Did you have a good time this week?'

I nod.

Nani's standing at the front door with the rest of the family, but nobody has come down to greet Dad at the car.

'Come up, Raju,' calls Nani. 'I've made chai.'

Kamaal goes off to park the car and Dad and Chloe wheel their suitcases over the bumpy ground, heaving them up the main steps.

'Sit, *beta*,' says Nani, taking Chloe's hand and guiding her to an armchair in the dining room where the whole family including Uma and Dev are crowded round.

Chloe stares at the garden beyond the French doors, the house, everything, like she's so impressed. 'Thank you. You are very kind for letting us stay the night.'

'And you sit too, Raju.' Nani's voice is clipped, like she's trying too hard to be nice.

Dad touches Nani's feet with his hands together. 'Thank you.'

Then it dawns on me that this must be the first time that Nani has seen Dad since I was born . . . or since Mum's funeral. I'm guessing they let him come to that?

Uma bustles in with a plate piled high with warm honeyed pastries. She brings them round to Dad's side and offers him one. 'You must be hungry after your big trip,' she says sweetly, half an eye on Nani. 'I remember how much you liked these.' She leans in and whispers, 'Remember how Chinty loved them too?'

'Thank you, Uma,' says Aunt Simran.

Dad is turning the colour of beetroot. He grabs one of the pastries and shoves it in his mouth. 'Thanks,' he says, taking a slurp of tea.

Chloe coughs. 'These are so yummy.' She takes a nibble and stares down at the floor.

'So where did Raju take you?' asks Aunt Simran. 'You are a photographer?'

'Yes,' replies Chloe. 'I mostly do portraits for magazines. *Harper's* and *Vogue*, you know?'

'Yes,' says Sufia, suddenly waking up and paying attention. 'I love those magazines.'

'But I wanted to see the Taj and all the sights. I took loads of great photos.' She waves her hands around. 'I can show you some of my magazine work if you like,' she says to Sufia. 'And I'd love to take some photos of this place too. It's quite something!'

'That would be lovely . . . we can show you round later,' says Sufia, twizzling her hair. 'Can't we, Tamarind?'

30

Later on, the sun is setting and the verandah looks amazing. Flower petals are scattered along the table and plates of steaming food are being laid between the tea lights.

Chloe finds me as I'm standing on the steps, looking out on to the garden, taking in the tamarind tree, trying to fix everything in my mind so I can remember it when I'm back in Bristol.

She puts a hand on my shoulder. 'I didn't want to startle you. I hope you had a good time, Tamarind. It's just that – it was my idea for you to come here.'

'Not Dad's?' I say, surprised.

'No . . . He didn't want to leave you, not really. He's been trying to protect you from everything . . . for too long. But I thought it was high time you got to know about your real mum.'

I don't know what to say.

'Sometimes you have to face the truth even if it hurts,' she continues. 'I hope you found the answers you were looking for . . . it's important.'

I clear my throat. 'It hasn't been easy, but I've got to know my family at last – thank you, Chloe.'

'I want you to know I'm not trying to take your mum's place. But I'm excited to be part of your life, Tam.'

I find myself reaching out for her and she wraps me in a hug. 'Me too,' I whisper in her ear.

Dad comes up behind and tickles us both. 'What are you two whispering about?'

'About you,' I joke. I leave them to chat and go and help Nani, who is polishing cutlery and counting the seats.

'Remember to lay a place for Papa,' says Arjun. 'He's coming back from his business trip today.'

'There's enough room for everyone,' says Nani, skirting around the grand velvet chair, not knowing what to do with it and finally pushing it in.

'Thank you for my party,' I say, looking at her tired face. 'I know this is hard for you.' I hold her hand.

'A beautiful party for my beautiful granddaughter. Now call everyone down, the food will get cold.'

Arjun, Sufia and me race upstairs. I keep tripping

over the skirt and would much rather have my jeans on, but I gather it into a bundle and call down the corridor, 'Dinner's ready.' We bang on all the bedroom doors, then chase each other back to the verandah.

'Got you,' says Arjun, laughing, catching hold of my skirt.

I'm out of breath and hold the stitch in my side. 'I'm going to miss you both.'

'Yeah. I'm going to miss you too,' says Arjun, pulling out a chair and collapsing on to it.

Dad and Chloe are already sitting down.

'Wow,' says Chloe. 'What a feast! This looks amazing.'

Uma brings more plates of hot food and Kamaal turns the music up. 'Let's get this party started,' he says, doing a silly dance.

Sufia looks happy and we exchange a quick look. She's really animated and chats away to Chloe, poring over her photos and laughing at something she says.

Maybe things are going to be OK after all.

'I baked you a special cake,' says Sufia, blushing as she points it out. 'It sank a bit in the middle but I just put more icing sugar on.'

'It's lovely – thank you.'

Uma has gone to town: there are plates of pastries sprinkled with green pistachios, wide bowls filled with red and orange fruits, little pink glasses with layered jellies, and swirls of thick cream.

'Thank you, Uma,' I say, giving her a big grin. 'It all looks amazing.'

'Happy birthday, Tamarind,' she says.

'Happy birthday,' everyone sings.

Dad looks over at my plate loaded up with pomegranate-sprinkled rice, a quarter of a potato *dhosa* and a *samosa* covered in *imilie* chutney. Not a scrambled egg in sight.

He raises his glass. 'Well well,' he says in a low voice.

I blush, feeling pleased with myself. 'I helped Uma make the *samosa* with a teeny sprinkle of chilli.'

We're just about to tuck into the food when a car pulls up and a man gets out.

'It's your Uncle Ruben,' says Nani.

'Papa,' shouts Arjun, leaping up. 'You're back.'

Uncle Ruben stands on the top step, jangling keys in his hand. His suit is crumpled and his tie is loose. He gives Arjun and Sufia a big hug. 'It was a long trip,' he says, glancing round the table. 'Good to see you, Tamarind.' He touches my cheek.

He doesn't say hi to Dad or Chloe. When he sees

191

Dad sitting there, he just stares. It's silent except for the thump-thump of the music and the rustling of the bunting in the breeze. Suddenly the atmosphere has changed completely – I feel cold and tense.

'I . . . I think we should all talk about what happened,' says Dad, shifting in his chair.

The silence continues and nobody else speaks.

'You were all mad with me and Chinty, I understand that. We were young, not married, but we would have, in time.' He looks at Chloe and she squeezes his hand. 'After we'd had the baby – I mean, Tamarind . . . sorry.' He crinkles his eyes at me.

'Go on, Dad.' I don't know where this bravery comes from, but I want to defend him and it's time I heard Dad's side of the story.

'You all know what Chinty was like. She had strong ideas, and she made me promise me that once she'd had Tamarind, we'd go on an adventure, the three of us. She wanted to move to England with me and she knew you – her family – didn't want that. So when things went so terribly wrong, she made me promise to take our baby and do the things we'd planned anyway. And then . . . you were all so angry.'

'I think we had a right to be,' says Uncle Ruben, clenching his fists by his side and glaring at Dad.

'You stole our niece, granddaughter and cousin away from us. She was all we had left of Chinty.'

Dad's face turns red, even the tips of his ears, but he carries on. 'I hurried away because I was scared you'd keep my baby from me – and I stayed away because you all hated me for it.' Dad pauses to swipe his cheeks. 'Because of that, I felt I couldn't bring Tamarind back. Chinty and I loved each other. And all these years I couldn't bring myself to tell Tamarind what really happened. I thought it was better to ignore it and cover it up. It was only when I met Chloe that I realized . . .'

I put my arms around Dad's neck – on the other side, Chloe is holding his hand. 'It's time we all stopped hurting each other,' I say, glancing up at Uncle Ruben. 'Mum would want it to end.' I look at Sufia and Nani. 'Thank you all for making me welcome and bringing me back into the family and thank you, Dad and Chloe, for bringing me home.' I fiddle with my star of Ishta ring. 'All these years I've wondered who I really am and for the first time, being here, even though it's been tough at times, I've started to find out about Mum. I've found things out that I never could have, without coming here.' I let the tears roll down my face. 'There's magic in the mountains, in the garden, the magic of my beautiful mum, Chinty. I know, wherever she is, she wants an end to this fighting.'

I feel Nani's hands on my shoulders. 'It's Tamarind's birthday – and every year I want her to come home. Instead of being sad about what we've lost, we're going to be happy for all that we still have – we have so much to celebrate. Everyone is welcome and that includes Raju and Chloe.'

For a minute I think Uncle Ruben is going to start a row, but instead he says, 'Ma is right. Welcome home, Tamarind. And welcome back, Raju.' The tension floods away from the table.

'Let's cut the cake,' shouts Arjun.

'And open your dad's presents, Tam!' says Sufia, pushing them towards me.

Uncle Ruben shuffles towards Dad. They don't speak but they shake hands. My face is stiff with salty streaks and I'm not sure if this truce will last or not, but at least they're trying, at least they've made a start.

The night has crept on to the verandah and it's brought with it the twinkling stars and cool fragrant air. There's a yellow glow from the fairy lights and the night frogs begin their gentle croaking.

I blow out the candles and make my wish.

No more fights ever, and Mum, please stay with me

now that I've found you. I hold the ring close inside my hand.

I don't really care about the presents – today has been exciting enough already – but I open them politely and put them to one side: the statue of the Taj Mahal, some glittery tea lights and my *adopt a tiger* certificate, all from Chloe and Dad.

Arjun, Sufia and me can't get out fast enough and walk into the tranquil garden. Arjun runs ahead.

'I'm sorry about Dad,' Sufia says.

'And mine.' I let out the breath that's been sitting tight in my chest. 'Dads, honestly.' I laugh and feel a bit better. 'Look,' I say, pointing at the evening star sitting snugly beside the moon, imagining Mum up there somewhere. 'It's Ishta and Chinty.'

We stay like that, not speaking, staring at the stars and listening to the wild calls of the animals beyond the garden for ages. 'I've had such a special time. This place is amazing and I can't wait to come back next year.'

'Me neither . . . and maybe Ishta will come too.'

'What are you two going on about?' asks Arjun, running back to us, breathless.

Sufia and I exchange a glance and I nod. Arjun's my friend, and it must've been tough being alone while everything with Ishta was going on. I'm happy to let him in on why I haven't been around so much. 'Arjun,' begins Sufia. 'You might not believe this, but since Tamarind arrived, she's woken up the wild garden and some incredible things have happened . . .'

We all sit on the damp grass under the blazing stars, and between me and Sufia we tell Arjun all about Ishta, Hanu her little monkey, Mum, and how my tamarind tree blossomed again.

'Wow,' says Arjun, his eyes so wide the whites almost glow in the night.

31

In the morning the sun bursts in through the shutters. Sufia is a real sleepyhead, and even though the sun is bright she doesn't stir.

I quietly step on to the floor and pull my suitcase from under the bed. I collect my things and begin to pack. I find the dinky little socks Nani gave me yesterday and hold them in my palm. I examine the silver rattle and look at the pictures in the storybook and then tuck everything – Mum's things from the hut, the album Sufia gave me, the bow and arrow and my baby box – safely between my clothes and close the suitcase.

I pick up Mum's photo from the side table, the one with the crease that I've carried all the way from Bristol, and hold it to my heart. I've got to know Mum at last and it gives me a warm feeling. I've found out more about her than I ever thought I would. I know she loved me, that she held me and soothed me, and that if she could, she would have stayed with me in this life.

And that even though she's gone, she's still here too – all around me.

I slot the photo safely in my pocket and feel happy that everything is out in the open, proud of myself that I did what Mum wanted me to and helped bring the family back together.

Sufia in the bed opposite finally blinks and lies half awake under the covers. 'Morning,' she mumbles.

'Morning.'

'Don't go . . . can't you stay a bit longer?'

I laugh. 'Of course I'd like to, especially now we're friends. Come on, lazy lops, get dressed then we can spend our last morning together.'

While Sufia splashes water in the bathroom, I fish out the arrow from my case and lay it on Sufia's bed.

She comes back to the bedroom and begins dressing. 'What's this?'

'I went back to the wild garden with Nani – I wanted to show her that the tamarind tree had blossomed again even after it was struck by lightning. I wanted her to believe in the magic of the garden and Mum. I found Mum's bow and arrow hidden under the fallen branches of the tree.' I pick up the bow from where it rests on top of my packing, padded with clothes to keep it safe. 'I want you to have Mum's arrow, then we both have some of her magic. They go together, see? Just like us.'

Sufia picks up the arrow carefully from her bed, running her finger along its length. 'It's beautiful. Thank you.'

I give her a long hug and take a final deep breath of Mum's bedroom. I fish the tamarind pod from my pocket and hold it against the sunlight, giving it a shake. 'Do you think if I planted this I could grow my own tamarind tree?'

'It's worth a try,' says Sufia. 'You never know.'

I place the seed pod and the bow under my clothes in the suitcase. 'I'll give it a go.'

Sufia finishes dressing. 'Chloe's really lovely. She said she'd help me with a work placement – I want to be a writer, you know – and I might even be able to come to uni in Bristol.'

'That would be amazing,' I say, putting a hand on Sufia's shoulder. 'And you can share my bedroom. I haven't been too kind to Chloe.' I feel my cheeks flush. 'But you're right – she *is* lovely.'

We run down the stairs and join the others for one final breakfast on the verandah.

'Let's go and help Uma bring the food in,' says Sufia, jumping up.

'Why don't you make some of your amazing origami animals and we can use them as place settings?' I say to Arjun. He's like a little brother and I don't want him feeling left out, since me and Sufia made up.

His face lights up. 'I'll go and get some paper.'

'Lovely having all your help,' says Uma as we scoot through to the kitchen where she has everything organized on the worktop.

I put my arms around her. 'Uma, you put so much effort into the food for me, thank you. You've worked so hard.'

'I have to make sure my food brings you back. I make the things I know you like – sweet tooth—'

'Just like Chinty!' Sufia and I giggle.

We carry the things out of the kitchen and bump into Uncle Ruben and Dad as we leave. They're patting each other on the back and joking around, heading out to the verandah.

'Everything's sorted now,' says Dad. 'I don't want you worrying about a single thing.'

Arjun has made everyone a different origami animal from coloured paper, the bunting still hangs in festive loops from the verandah ceiling and the sun is sparkling through the trees, bathing everything in golden light.

Dad, Uncle Ruben, Kamaal and Arjun take their

seats around a circular side table. In the middle a plate with chillies is laid ready, like green and red wheel spokes.

'Everyone up for the famous Himalayan chilli challenge?' laughs Uncle Ruben, picking a narrow dark-green chilli.

Dad gives me a wink. 'We did this at university.' He picks a small one. 'No sweat.'

Me and Sufia giggle at them and shuffle the dishes along the table before sitting down.

'I know you might not do the chilli challenge this time,' says Arjun, putting a small rectangular package on the table, 'but I made you some chilli chocolate to take away with you.'

'Oh, wow! Thank you – promise I'll practise.' He's even tied a ribbon round it. 'You're the best, and when you come to Bristol I'll take you to the suspension bridge – you'll love it.'

Uma brings in a jug of *lassi* and puts it down at the far end before squeezing in beside Arjun.

'Come on,' says Nani, beckoning to the others, who leave the chilli challenge and join the main table. 'Tuck in, everyone.'

A sudden breeze in the garden makes us all stop eating and look up.

'It's Hanu,' I cry, running down the steps to where

the little monkey is waiting at the bottom, as if long-ing to be invited up to eat with the rest of us.

He takes my hand and I lead him to the table.

'Oh,' says Nani. 'Chinty had a golden monkey just like him.'

Hanu jumps on to the blue velvet chair, the one Nani didn't let anyone sit at before, and claps his hands.

Nani stands by Hanu and peers at him. 'Can it be you, little Hanu?' she asks, tickling him under the chin. 'We haven't seen him for so long, I can't be sure. He's quite an old monkey now!'

He grabs the pomegranate in Nani's hand as if to say 'how rude!' and begins chomping into it.

'Cheeky as ever,' laughs Nani, her eyes shining. 'Welcome home, Hanu. You will always have a place at the table just like before, on Chinty's chair.'

'Hurray!' cries Arjun, sliding in with Hanu on Mum's special chair and giving Hanu a hug. 'I'll look after you.'

'Here's to all of us,' says Uncle Ruben.

'And may we all sit together at this table for many, many years to come,' says Aunt Simran.

We all clap and raise our glasses.

'That's it,' says Nani, going about the table hugging everyone. *One big happy family.*

LETTER FROM THE AUTHOR

The inspiration for this story came from my mum. Her own mother died when she was young and so she never really knew her, but I think she felt her loss all through her life. I wanted to create a magical, almost mythological setting full of imagination for the place where a missing mother could be found. When I began sketching and pondering about where this place might be, straight away I knew I wanted to create another story set in the Himalaya with a secret garden. Inspired by our dear monkey Oma, who lived on the family farm in India with us, I was thrilled to finally write a monkey into my story.

My Indian heritage holds the belief that people's spirits continue to live after them, and in Tamarind's story I wanted to use this as a way to give and show hope.

I carried out lots of research for the novel and discovered the beautiful story of the Mesopotamian goddess Ishtar, the evening and morning star and the predecessor to the goddess Venus. In the way that only happens to those of us who believe in the magical, every day when I wrote this book, the star of Ishtar sparkled from my window as brightly as she could, and I knew she had to be part of my story. Ishtar can be visited at the British Museum. Ask to be shown to the Queen of the Night!

Jasbinder Bilan 2020

The spellings of Hindi and Punjabi words used throughout Tamarind & the Star of Ishta *are the ones used by Jasbinder's family when she was growing up in India.*

ACKNOWLEDGEMENTS

Firstly, of course, huge thanks to my wonderful mum, Gurjinder, who is the one who brings our family together and nurtures us with cooking and love. To my dearest grandmother Chinty whose name I have brought to life in this story, you are always in my heart. My husband Ian and my sons Gem and Satchen, who continue to be patient and keep bringing tea, cakes and love at regular intervals so I can perform my writing marathons. To my enthusiastic siblings, Balraj, Sherry, Randhiraj, Dip and Amolack, who keep waving the victory flags. To the next generation of the Bilan family: Avarni, Jyodh, Arran, Ashari, Rajan, Xanthe, Tara, Rubuen, Rani, Evan, Jadan, Arron and Aneve. To my dear Judy for all our memories.

The team at Chicken House have been so wonderful throughout my debut year. Thank you for all the celebrations – cake, tea, champagne and glitz at the Costas, you kept my feet firmly in the clouds! Huge thanks to the magical Barry Cunningham for asking me to write more stories. To my fantastic editor Kesia who really is a total star when it comes to suggesting ways to make things better and more beautiful. Your insight and skill have been at the heart of reshaping this story. When one editor isn't enough, in steps the wonderful Rachel Leyshon with a sprinkle of questions, suggestions and glitter. Rachel H for creating another heart-stopping cover and to Studio Helen and Aitch for the stunning artwork. Thank you to Jazz for all your support and confidence this year in helping me to navigate the publicity machine (looking forward to our Himalayan leg!). To Laura, Esther and Sarah for waving a wand and turning my typed story into an actual book. And to the fabulous Elinor Bagenal for taking my books across the seas.

To my agent Ben for his unbounding enthusiasm, for always being there on the end of the phone to offer advice or anything else I need, and for loving Tamarind.

Carolyn Rayner's artful eye made sure that my

website and book posts kept zinging with creativity. Thank you for all your hard work.

Writing can often be a lonely activity, so it is hugely important to have friends who will drop everything to meet for coffee, champagne . . . even writing sometimes! Mel and Miranda have been with me since the very start and they truly are the dream team. Thank you for your wisdom and for always being right. To my dear friend Rachael for all her love and support and to her daughters Bel and Minti. Thank you, Kate L. My very own equine goddess and beautiful spirit.

To all the staff and pupils at my Patron of Reading school (my old school), the ever impressive Mellers Primary in Nottingham, where my love of reading and creativity were nurtured by the fantastic Mr Ferrigan, Mr Stanton and Mrs Wallis. To my Year 6 'fans' at Mellers: Jack, Daisha, Taniayah, Anas, Ayaan, Aisosa, Milan, Romeo, Murtaza, J'Maer, Mayar, Rayan and Mariyah – I've had such fun visiting you and discussing reading. You are all superstars. Thank you especially for your help with building Arjun's character and for all your amazing suggestions – good luck at big school, you are going to smash it!

It has been such an honour to be part of Nottingham City of Literature – thank you for all the opportunities and I can't wait to step inside the new magnificent biggest children's library in the UK!

Thank you to the Society of Authors for their generosity in awarding me a work-in-progress grant. Thank you also to Paper Nations for selecting me for the Time to Write commission. To the wonderful MA Creative Writing for Young People Course at Bath Spa University for their continuing support and finally to Costa for awarding me the Children's Book Award 2019.

Heartfelt thanks to all the teachers, librarians, booksellers and reviewers for championing my stories. Special thanks to: Inspire ELS, Imogen Russell Williams, Florentyna Martin, Alex O'Connell, Lauren St John, Sita Bramachari, the amazing Mr E and Kate Rundell for your kindness and support. And finally to you, my readers, who I can't wait to take on more adventures . . . Where shall we go next?

Photo by Ian Sharp

According to family stories, Jasbinder Bilan was born in a stable close to the foothills of the Himalaya. Until she was a year and a half, she lived on a farm inhabited by a grumpy camel and a monkey called Oma.

Jasbinder grew up in Nottingham, and now lives in a wooded valley close to Bath with her husband, two teenage boys and dog Enzo. She has an MA in Creative Writing for Young People from Bath Spa University, and splits her time between teaching and writing.

Asha & the Spirit Bird, Jasbinder's debut novel, won the Times Children's Fiction Competition 2017 and the Costa Children's Book Award 2019, was nominated for the Carnegie Medal 2020, was longlisted for the Jhalak Prize 2020, and is shortlisted for the Waterstones Book Prize 2020.

jasbinderbilan.co.uk
@jasinbath

ASHA & THE SPIRIT BIRD

Asha lives in the foothills of the Himalayas. Money is tight and she misses her papa who works in the city. When he suddenly stops sending his wages, a ruthless moneylender ransacks their home and her mother talks of leaving.

From her den in the mango tree, Asha makes a pact with her best friend, Jeevan, to find her father and make things right. But the journey is dangerous: they must cross the world's highest mountains and face hunger, tiredness – even snow leopards.

And yet, Asha has the unshakeable sense that the spirit bird of her grandmother – her nanijee – will be watching over her.

'This book is such a light-filled, huge-hearted delight of an adventure.'
KATHERINE RUNDELL

Paperback, ISBN 978-1-911490-19-7, £6.99 • ebook, ISBN 978-1-911490-78-4, £6.99